Cherry Pie

SOTIA LAZU

Other Books in This Series
Cherry Pop (Vampire Cherry Book 0)
Cherry Stem (Vampire Cherry Book 1)
Cherry Blossom (Vampire Cherry Book 2)

For those who don't know what they want but recognize it
when they have it

Table of Contents

Prologue

"Cherry, can't you see he's lying through his teeth? I can, and I'm on a different continent."

Alex had his reasons for being suspicious, but Constantine wasn't lying. Things would have been much easier if he were.

I wouldn't have to die again.

But I'm starting the story in the middle.

Let me fix that.

Chapter One

I open myself to the scenery around me, until the stitches holding it together glow a pure white. The sunglasses holding my hair back from my face are useless against this light, but I don't want to dim it, anyway. I need to take it in.

The sight is beautiful in its eeriness.

I focus on a single point along the seam between golden sand and blue morning sky. About where the overhead light switch should be. It doesn't give, but it will. I've been practicing since I was trapped in Alex's dream.

I use my finger to draw a bright-red thread over it, and snap it with my finger. I tug, and my strawberry daiquiri fades to transparency before it's gone completely. The book on my lap follows it to oblivion. The wind has dropped, and the waves no longer lap at the shore. They're frozen in place until I pull again, and then they melt into the sky that in turn gives its place to the white of my bedroom walls.

I close my eyes and smile when the beach chair beneath me yields into something softer. Fluffier. I open my eyes again and—

I blinked away my much-needed sleep. Did Constantine have to drop into my dream tonight of all nights? His timing sucked.

Speaking of timing, I should start keeping track of how long it took to enter and exit a dream. I practiced every chance I got and was improving—another reason I was so tired; I needed to let my mind switch off once in a while—but I wanted tangible results.

Maybe I'd ignore my ex's new bout of drama and sink back into my dream.

Sure.

I'd forget he said I could be human again, so I could catch some shut eye. 'Cause I was cool like that.

Not.

I kicked the sheets off and stood. My inner clock told me the sun was still down for the count, which meant so were my parents. I didn't want to sneak out of their home without saying *goodbye*, but if what Constantine said was true, I couldn't wait to get more details out of him.

I pulled on my jeans and sneakers, and wore my hoodie over Alex's T-shirt I'd been using as a pajama top. His scent was barely there after ten days. I didn't know where we stood, other than that we weren't a *we*, but I liked feeling close to him at night. And it was a comfy shirt.

I scribbled a quick note for my parents on a Post-It and pressed it to the fridge door with the heel of my hand.

Constantine needs me at the mansion. I'll be back
tomorrow, for my stuff and a proper farewell.
And I'll need pancakes. Lots of them.

Love you both,
Cherry

It was a three-and-a-half-hour drive back to L.A. without traffic, but traffic didn't apply to me and neither did driving. I was flying there. I pulled my hair into a tight bun and raised the hood, to minimize damage, and took off.

The crisp night air felt refreshing on my skin and called up memories of the warmth of the dream. The heat had been at its strongest when Constantine was there.

And when wasn't that the case?

As trees and hills gave way to wide open road beneath me, my mind flew forward, to the mansion and the man waiting there.

Constantine didn't reach out before tonight, respecting my time with my family. I appreciated that, but until I dreamed of him topless beside me, I hadn't realized I'd missed him. It was weird. We broke up years ago, but the last few months he'd been a constant in my life, and I liked having him around.

Another thing to sort out if I wanted a future with Alex.

Which I did.

With the exception of his… dark period, Alex was the *yang* to Constantine's *yin*. He was open with his feelings, unafraid of commitment, and with a moral compass so strong, you could count on him to always draw a clear line between right and wrong.

Constantine was all about gray areas and fuzzy limits.

And I was confused.

Not about which of them to choose. Constantine was history—though who knows what would have happened between us if Ádísa hadn't planned and executed our breakup?

Not what I should be considering.

The hazy scenery beneath me gained shape. I cut into the smog, thankful I didn't have to breathe. I began my descent, careful to keep away from the lights. Not easy in downtown L.A. but doable around Constantine's mansion.

My feet met solid ground at the same time, and I brought my body to a perfect halt. Can I get a *yay* for bending the laws of physics?

I lowered my hood and let my hair loose. It felt stiff, and I bet it looked it, but this wasn't a social call.

Constantine said I could become human again.

How?

And why wasn't I ringing his doorbell and asking him?

I pressed the button by the wrought-iron gate and smiled at the closed circuit camera, waiting for Wesley, Constantine's aging human butler, to buzz me in. Flying all the way to someone's front door unannounced is considered an aggressive move among our kind, but I wasn't afraid Constantine would see it as such. I was simply being polite. He was waiting for me, but I wasn't staying here yet. Or again. Or at all, depending on how our chat went.

"Come to the parlor. We'll watch the sunrise." Constantine's voice came from behind me, instead of from my left, where the intercom was.

I spun on my heel. Nothing. The acoustics out here were wonky.

The latch clicked, and the gate slid open. "I didn't come for the sunrise," I muttered under my breath, though I couldn't wait to see it. Couldn't get enough sun since my grandmother's potion made it possible for me to walk in daylight. If only I could tan…

I followed the path to the front door and let myself in. Wesley poked his head out of the kitchen, and a smile brightened his lined face. He looked tired. I couldn't blame him; he'd been taking care of too many people for a while now.

"You've been missed," he said. "Coffee?"

"I missed you too." I returned the smile. "And yes, please." No need to tell him how I took it; he'd made me coffee more times than I could count, both when I dated Constantine and in the months Alex and I stayed here.

I padded softly on the plush carpet, as I trailed through the ground floor, praying I met nobody else before I talked to Constantine. I'd love to catch up with Sheena, and the little masochist in me missed the three fledglings

Constantine sort of adopted on the day he decapitated his maker, but I could do without diversions until I had answers.

From past experience, odds were Constantine would be less than fully dressed, so I wasn't surprised to see him in nothing but a pair of silk pajama bottoms. I crossed the threshold to the spacious parlor at the exact same moment the rising sun appeared through the glass panes taking up three sides of the room. The rays that a couple weeks ago would have reduced Constantine to ashes now set his pale skin ablaze with red, orange, and purple hues. The muscles in his wide sternum stood out in stark relief, and his blue eyes sparkled.

He was magnificent.

I didn't try to hide my ogling. He expected it. It wouldn't surprise me if he'd timed my entrance specifically for this.

I blinked, and whatever thrall he held over me evaporated. He was still stunning, but now I could focus on things beyond that. "You said I could become human again?" I asked.

"I did."

I was looking right at him, but I didn't see him move his lips.

"Finally, she catches on. I've been dropping hints for a while." His lips never parted.

"How are you doing this? Are you messing with my mind?"

He held my gaze. "I've broken my promise," he said, and this time I watched him form the words. His serious tone was a far cry from the seductive purr he usually opted for when shirtless. "I've kept something important from you."

Ah, now I got it. "How long have you known I could be turned back?" I glared. Would he never learn? Omissions and lies always came back to bite him in the ass. And I wouldn't think of that thing's perfect curve.

"No. Not that. I informed you of the possibility as soon as Ruby told me about it. There's something else." His mouth stopped moving, but the words kept coming. "*When two vampires who've killed their own makers exchange blood, they get a sort of telepathy.*"

Shock and surprise short-circuited my brain.

"*I killed Ádísa, and you killed Willoughby,*" he said. In my head. "*And then—*"

"You cleaned my wounds and fed me your blood. Three times."

"*Yes. And you don't have to speak aloud. I can hear your thoughts.*"

This was too fucking much. He'd crossed lines and pushed my limits time and again, but to be able to straight-up pull thoughts out of my head? No. "You do that, and I promise to hurt you so bad, you'll taste it for eternity. My thoughts are mine. No trespassing. Got it?" I refused to use my inside voice.

"*Cherry, I would never disrespect you this way. You have to believe me.*"

"Do I?" I was tired of believing him. Of trusting him. More tired of reminding myself not to. "Don't tell me you only found out about this now, too." Oh, he knew for a while.

He'd insisted on giving me *his* blood when Alex tried to feed me.

"No." He said this aloud. "I've known for years, and after Alex… After you were hurt the first time, I couldn't overlook the opportunity."

"To bind me to you?" I asked. The arrogance was strong with this one.

He frowned. "Of course not. To never let you get hurt again. Wherever you are, whatever happens, you'll be able to reach me at the speed of thought. Think about this, Cherry." His eyes pleaded with me to forgive him, and I found myself wanting to.

"You should've let me choose for myself." I was tired of people thinking they knew what was best for me.

"You were drained. There was no time to discuss it."

"You could have come to me later."

"I didn't think that far ahead." He stood and scratched his chest, his bicep bulging. He used his body as a distraction, but I knew all his tricks, and they wouldn't work this time.

"You're lying," I said. "You jumped at the chance to have an in with me, and you knew it when you told Alex you wouldn't be my default choice. Games. It's all about games with you."

His blue eyes darkened to near black, as he narrowed them at me. "There was nothing game-like about seeing you drained in your parents' basement, with your crazed lover still inside you, and knowing I could have prevented it. You'd be dead now if I didn't act."

I arched an eyebrow. "Alex might have stopped."

"You don't believe that any more than I do, but I'm not talking about then. How do you think I found you in that clearing?" Where Willoughby made Alex bleed me out.

I remembered wondering about that at the time, before more pressing matters had demanded my attention. Like surviving. "But you hadn't had my blood then. You only licked my wounds clean after," I said.

"When I gave you my blood the first time, I held you. Your blood was all over me, driving me insane. I knew the effects wouldn't last if I only tasted it, so I went for it." He raked his fingers through his long blond hair.

"And at the clearing?"

He held my gaze. "You'd almost died twice, Cherry. I wouldn't leave it to chance. I took enough to know this bond would last. That I wouldn't lose you again."

I should be livid. He'd made the decision for me. Twice. *To protect me.* As if I were a helpless little girl, and not a vampire who could stand on her own two feet—and kick ass, when need arose.

But his last words… His eyes, swirling with color that I knew corresponded to pain and hunger and even love…

He didn't want to lose me, and more than once he'd gone above and beyond, to keep me safe and happy.

I closed the distance between us and touched my lips to his cheek. *"I forgive you."* I tried to think it at him, unsure how this worked.

He slid his hands up my arms, his touch lighting my skin on fire. When he reached my shoulders, he dug in his fingers, holding me to him. *"I'll make you happy, if it kills me."*

The emotion in his words slammed into my chest and made me lightheaded. It took all my willpower not to think of a response. I couldn't trust myself not to project it to him, and I didn't know what it would be, when my gut reaction was to lose myself in him.

But that way lay badness.

He nuzzled my cheek. "I made so many mistakes as your mentor. I fancied myself a sort of Pygmalion and tried to sculpt the perfect woman out of you, when I should have spent our time together letting you know you already were perfect. *Are* perfect."

He'd approached me as my VSS-assigned mentor and had done his best to teach me all he could, but I never shook the feeling he found me lacking. That I couldn't compare to the Valkyrie who made him. My insecurities intensified when he cheated on me with her, and they didn't go away even when he killed her for me.

He'd said he loved me—before and since—but this validation filled my stomach with butterflies.

"You really think I'm perfect?" I whispered against his ear.

He shifted to touch his forehead to mine. "You're beautiful, and you're smart. Funny and brave. A hellcat, in and out of bed. And your heart… This world has broken you down and stomped all over you, people have hurt you and betrayed you, and you *still* see the good in them. You see the good in me. Fuck yes, you're perfect." And then, with the slightest tilt of his head, he found my lips and claimed them.

Soft, full lips glided against mine, before his talented tongue slid between them and caressed my own. I melted against him, my heart absorbing his words. I skated my palms up his sides, enjoying the hardness of muscle beneath his smooth skin.

It was incredible.

I was kissing Constantine again, after so long. After I was sure he and I were done.

When I'd been thinking of another man.

I said I wouldn't wait for Alex, but part of me wanted us to fix things. To regain the normal, easy relationship we had before Willoughby and Ádísa threw us the mother of all curveballs.

With great reluctance and even greater regret, I broke the kiss. "Too soon," I said.

He ghosted his thumb over my cheek. "Will it ever not be?"

I had no reply for that. "Is it okay if I stay here?" I asked after a second.

"Of course." His smile lit up the room.

"And you'll tell me about the whole vampire-to-human reversion thing?"

The smile wilted. When it reappeared, it didn't reach his eyes. "Anything to make you happy."

Chapter Two

I took a sip of the coffee Wesley brought me, and bit back a moan of appreciation. His brew could wake the dead—I vouched for it.

"I'm ready," I said. "Tell me everything."

Constantine nodded. "My last year as a human, I was one of a select army of Viking warriors, sent to guard the Byzantine emperor Vasilios the Second. It was the late tenth century, and we were known as the Varangian Guard." He'd reverted to his most cultured tone, the one unaffected by me and the three vampettes who taught him things like *OMG* and *WTF*.

He cleared his throat. "During the battle of Abydos—you might know it as Hellespont—"

I wouldn't know it as anything; I had no clue whether it was a place or an artifact. Plus, I was still doing the math, to calculate his exact age. He'd been turned in his early thirties, so… I'd always thought of him as ancient, but I guess he was only eleven hundred years old or so. *Only.*

"—we were fighting the rebel Bardas Phokas, when a sword sliced through my side. I dispatched of my attacker and was forced to seek shelter in the catacombs of a monastery. There, among the robes of a deceased priest, I found a scroll. At the time, I didn't know what its significance was, but I held on to it nonetheless."

I arched my eyebrows. "You were wounded and in a place filled with dead people, and you decided to keep a piece of paper that meant nothing to you?"

"*Parchment*, Cherry. It was old, and it called to me." He gave a rueful smile. "And it was in my hand when I died."

I leaned forward. "That's when Ádísa turned you?" I ached to reach for him and was grateful for the coffee table acting as a barrier between us. Touching him again wouldn't lead to good things. Correction—it'd probably lead to great things, which would be bad.

"Indeed. I remember the cold stone beneath me and the smell of mold in the air. When she leaned over me, I was sure she was a Valkyrie, come to take me to Valhalla."

She'd cultivated that myth for a while. Before I dusted her childe and co-conspirator, Willoughby, I found out she was really a succubus, who lost the Devil's favor when she fell for a mortal and failed to get his soul.

"What was Ádísa doing there?" I asked.

"She thrived on war. She joined the guard looking for blood and mayhem."

"But—" *She was a woman*, was what I meant to say. I must have thought it too loudly.

"Viking women never shied from battle."

"Makes sense." I could picture her slaying people, running them through with a sword, or tearing into them with her bare hands.

Constantine's gaze was vacant, as if he'd been transported to that time so long ago. "She was beautiful and fierce, and when she offered me immortality, I didn't refuse her. She sealed my wound, her lips cold against my fevered skin. She closed her mouth over my throat, and I wouldn't mind dying in her arms. I hadn't felt a woman's touch since I left my wife behind."

The shocks wouldn't stop coming. "You were married?"

He sighed. "I never saw her or my two daughters again. Never went back. I was dead and reborn that night. I buried my name together with my past." His eyes were dark and stormy with pain.

"Do you want to talk about it?"

He shook his head. "I loved them. I left. I died. I expect so did they."

I wouldn't press for more. This was his story to share.

"When I woke up, I was disoriented and ravenous. She fed me her blood and we spent the night together. I was enthralled by her beauty and ruthlessness. We joined the fight side by side and fed on our enemies and our warriors alike. By the time the battle was done and Phokas was dead, I was so taken with her, I'd have done anything she asked.

"You know the rest. I did her bidding for years. I followed her like her trained guard dog. We fought and parted ways for decades at a time, only to pick up where we'd left off. We traveled the world. Witnessed the wonders of technology. Broke up and reunited. Blood and death followed her. I didn't approve of senseless slaughter—no honor in that—but I didn't object. She was my everything, even when there was an ocean between us."

I *did* know this part, from bits and pieces he'd shared about his past the year and a half we'd been together, but I'd never heard this condensed version that showed how important she'd been to him. How deep his feelings for her ran. It wasn't jealousy I felt; in the end, he'd proven he loved me more. Hearing him talk about her with such awe, though, made me hurt for his loss and the hard choice he had to make when he killed her to save me.

"Society changed," Constantine said. "The need to hide our nature became more pronounced, but Ádísa was as reckless as ever. I cleaned her messes because I felt I had to, but as time went by, I became more vocal about questioning her decisions. And then there was Ruby."

My grandma, whom Ádísa left behind for dead and Constantine turned.

"And then there was me," I said.

Constantine's smile was brighter than the sun. "And then there was you." The warmth in his voice tugged at my very core.

I refused to meet his gaze. He's the only vampire I know whose eyes change color to match his emotions, and I didn't trust myself to resist what I'd see there. "Tell me about the scroll." My voice came out gruff and throaty.

He sat back and steepled his fingers on his stomach. "It was torn, but the part I found read, *they can walk under the sun and count finite remaining sunsets once again, requiring breath and sustenance, and growing as nature and God meant Man to.* At the time, I thought it was a blessing. Maybe part of a Christian Orthodox psalm. I knew nothing of their religion.

"I kept my piece in a box, alongside my Viking shield and sword, but never thought to look more into it. When Ruby came to my dream, she told me she'd found a translation of an ancient script in the Romanian mountains. It mentioned a way to revive a specific type of Strigoi, as they call vampires. The latter part of the text matches what I found in Abydos, and it seems it would work on us."

Well, hello, new information. "Us?"

He looked at his fingers. "It speaks about two immortals who've killed the ones who made them, assuming our understanding is correct." His voice was low.

"You're hiding something," I said.

"Not hiding. I'm merely savoring the next part."

I arched an eyebrow. "Spill."

He raised his head to face me. "The ritual involved calls for mutual draining"—mischief danced in his eyes and on his smirk—"during intercourse."

I laughed. The man knew how to relieve tension.

"I'm absolutely serious, I'm afraid," Constantine said. "Though if this is your reaction to the thought of us having sex, I have my work cut out for me."

I was wrong. No tension relieved, and now mental images of Constantine fucking my brains out came to add horniness on top of my stress. "You're serious," I half-said, half-asked.

He gave a slow nod. "It could be worse."

"Yeah. Could involve ritual sacrifice."

"In a way, it does." He frowned. "We're supposed to drink from one another until we both die."

"But then we're reborn."

His shrug was noncommittal. "Have you told your parents you're moving back here?"

"I left a note. I'll fly back tomorrow and get my stuff. Say a proper *goodbye*." Unlike last time, when I had no clue they knew about vampires, and I let them wait for my undead ass for more than six years.

"I'll join you," he said. "But for now, you should get some sleep. We have a long day ahead of us tomorrow. I suppose you'll want to be back in time to see Sheena and the girls off."

Huh? "*Off*, where?"

"They're moving out tomorrow evening. I'm sure we'll be reeled in to help with the last of their stuff."

"They're moving out? You didn't say anything."

"I thought Sheena did. You certainly talked a lot more to her than to me during your absence." *That* didn't sound whiny at all. "They made arrangements while we were in San

Louis Obispo. Your chatty friend is returning to her modeling agency and offered to take on the young ladies as clients. Take them in too, I suppose, since she invited them to stay at her place. I didn't think to mention it, because it wasn't about me and it didn't fall into the things-that-affect-you category."

He was right. It didn't affect me. Except for the part where he and I would be left in his sexy mansion with no buffer between us other than an aging human butler. Once the women were gone, Constantine might start running around the mansion without a stitch on. That thought brought back memories of him naked, gleaming in the candlelight as he hovered over me, a wicked smile on his lips, and his blue eyes swirling with violet.

Which made me realize—"You changed the subject."

"I did not." He sounded scandalized, to say the least, so I was pretty certain it was an act.

"You so did. You said we had to drink from each other until we died, and then I said we'd be reborn, and you changed the freaking subject. You promised you wouldn't hide anything else to do with me. *Promised.* Repeatedly." That he'd had reason to do so more than once should've taught me something about his credibility.

Constantine rolled his shoulders and straightened in his seat. When he looked at me, there was no humor in his gaze. "I don't want to tell you."

"Great. Now I *have* to know."

"This is about me. Not you."

I tilted my head to the side and studied his posture. His back was stiff, his shoulders square. His knuckles were even paler than the rest of him. "Is it about the ritual?" I asked.

"Yes."

"Tell me."

"You should decide on your own whether you will return to your human nature or not."

"Tell me," I said again.

He huffed and stood in a fluid motion that had the satin of his pants clinging to him and defining every curve.

"Your ass isn't going to take my mind off this," I told his sculpted back when he turned to look outside.

"This ritual will make us as old as we'd be if we were never turned."

I wasn't sure if he spoke the words or thought them at me, but they chilled me to the core. "That'll make me thirty, but you... You will be—"

"Gone."

I was up and in his face—yes, sandwiched between him and the floor-to-ceiling glass—in no time. "And you didn't think that affects me? Were you not going to tell me at all? I'd wake up human, covered in your fucking dust?" I didn't know what shocked me more—the fact that he'd keep this from me, or the searing agony twisting my gut at the thought of losing him forever. Not too long ago, I'd convinced myself I no longer cared if he lived or died.

"Cherry..."

"No. Fuck you. No." I was crying.

He wrapped his arms around me. "I don't know what I was going to do," he said. "I've been trying to think of a way out, but if there isn't one… You never wanted this life, and I've lived a dozen lifespans. Maybe it's my time."

"No. We're not doing this. You're not dying for me. And you're a bastard for even considering it." I shook off his hold and smacked his chest with my open palm.

He took a step back, and I felt cold. Weird. Vampires don't feel cold, unless we're talking arctic temperatures.

"I thought it was kind of romantic," he said with a shit-eating grin.

I scowled. "Jackass."

"Chivalrous, even."

"Asshole." But a smile tugged at the corners of my lips.

"Yeah, I love you too."

The words were spoken lightly, but they landed like a punch to my stomach. He really did. I believed him before, but now I felt it in my core. And it left me shaken.

"We should get some sleep," I said. I'd adjusted to a human schedule for the past ten days, but being a vampire in L.A. was much easier by night, and I'd apparently remain a bloodsucker after all.

Plus, it was a solid excuse to stop looking into Constantine's soulful eyes.

Chapter Three

It was well after noon, when Constantine and I left for my parents' house. The sun was no longer an issue, but onlookers were, so we couldn't fly there in the middle of the day. Alex had left his car at the mansion, and Constantine suggested we drive.

I shouldn't have agreed.

I hadn't seen Constantine drive since he took me to his place from the Vampire Social Services, early in my unlife. Memories of the debauchery that followed that ride combined with mental images of Alex behind the wheel—or fucking me on the hood, parked outside his mother's house—and amplified the awkward silence between Constantine and me. It was odd, being with him and not talking, but I didn't know what to say.

I leaned against the passenger door, seeking out a semblance of space. It didn't work. I felt Constantine's presence as vividly as if we were pressed together.

Maybe it was the ultra-naughty Constantine-centered dream I had during my beauty sleep. I was able to change it more than once, but my stubborn subconscious fleeted back to him every single time.

Did he insinuate his way into my dreams?

Was he reading my thoughts this very moment?

No. He said he wouldn't, and I'd drive myself crazy if I second-guessed that.

I studied him. He wore jeans and a form fitting T-shirt that had become the norm *after* he and I broke up. While we dated, he was always impeccably dressed and coiffed, but I liked this hair-in-the-wind version more.

His triceps bunched as he shifted gear, and I licked my lips. *Shit.* Better pray for no traffic.

It was a frigging long three-and-a-half hours, and I pretended to sleep through much of it, when I wasn't commenting on the weather.

Mom and Dad were inordinately excited to see Constantine. There was hugging and kissing and pointed looks, rife with innuendo. No pancakes, though.

Once we were done packing and loading the car, Mom ignored my glares and invited us to stay the night.

"It's almost seven, and it *is* a long drive," Constantine said. "It may be a good idea."

It wasn't. Our rooms at the mansion weren't right next to each other. Here, we'd sleep a few feet apart—and

Constantine slept in the buff. It was different when I had Alex in bed with me and a threat hung over our heads. Now there would be little to keep my mind occupied.

Luckily, there was a valid reason for us to go back to L.A. tonight. "We can't stay." I tried to sound sorry. "We promised to help the girls with their move."

"Indeed." The look Constantine gave me said he saw right through me. "But there is time for a cup of coffee, and Cherry has some news for you."

Damn it.

I didn't want to get my parents' hopes up, when I saw no way around the pesky issue of needing to sacrifice Constantine to regain my humanity.

"Really?" Mom ushered us to the kitchen and started the coffee maker.

Dad sliced up some cake and joined us at the table. It was all so mundane and normal. I could have that. I slid my gaze to Constantine. *No.* The price was too high.

He smiled. "Go on."

"Constantine may have found a way for me to become human again," I said.

The mug Mom held clanked against the counter. She looked at me, and the hope I meant to avoid shone in her eyes.

It hurt that I had to squash it. "It's not easy, and we don't know if it's even possible."

"It's possible," Constantine said.

Dad reached across the table and covered my hand with his. "Whatever makes you happy makes us happy. We'll love you the same, fangs or no fangs."

I wanted to fly into his arms. Instead, I turned my palm and gave his hand a squeeze. "We'll look into it more. I'll let you know what we find out, but it may not happen."

Constantine shrugged. He took the coffee my mom offered and pulled out a chair for her. "We'll do our best to see it does."

Maybe I didn't mind him dying, after all. I was minutes from staking him where he sat.

A short and awkward conversation later—I mean, what plans *could* I have for the future, Dad?—I was beyond ready to go.

More hugging and kissing and promising to keep in touch, all with a knot in my throat. This *goodbye* wasn't permanent. It didn't have to be a long one either; I could see them every weekend now on. I still wished I could stay with them a while longer. I was supposed to spend a couple months in my childhood home with a little R-n-R, gorging on Mom's food without worrying about calories, and no boy drama. What more could I ask for?

Oh right. To be human again. And I couldn't have that either, without costing Constantine his unlife. *Boo.*

Mom stuffed the trunk of the car with bottles of Ruby's brew. "I've kept some too, just in case," she said.

Constantine gathered her in a hug. "Thank you, Kathleen. If things work out, our little Gertrude won't need it for long," he said.

I didn't know whether to slap him for promising things he couldn't deliver or for using my given name which I'd rather forget.

The moment the car doors were closed and my parents couldn't hear, I plastered a smile on my face and whispered, "Will you stop doing that?"

"What?" Constantine waved at Mom and Dad and peeled off the driveway.

"Making them believe it's possible to have their daughter back."

"You *are* their daughter."

"You know what I'm saying. You let them think I'll be human again."

He shook his head, gaze on the road. "After all this time, you have no faith in my problem-solving abilities."

"I have every faith on your problem-creating abilities, if that helps."

"It doesn't." He sounded sad, which shouldn't bother me but did.

"You said yourself I can only go back if I drain you to dust. That's not an option."

This time, he turned to look at me. "I may have a solution to that."

Now I was the one getting my hopes up. I waited for him to say more. When he didn't, I asked, "Care to elaborate?"

"I've been reading the text in a way that made sense to me, but I was wrong. For both of us to turn human, we must be *consumed*, but not necessarily consume each other.

What if I drain you, while you feed from someone else to keep from dusting?"

Someone else who'd be in the room while Constantine and I had sex? "Do you have someone in mind?"

He didn't hesitate. "Alex. He's of your bloodline. It may be an acceptable cheat, and if it doesn't work, there's no real loss."

We'd both still be around. Still vampires.

There was one tiny problem. "How do we pitch that to Alex?"

"Preferably over video chat." Constantine chuckled. "I need to be able to see his face."

Two hours into the drive, I was hungry, and not for blood. I craved something greasy and calorie ridden, to drown out the fantasies wreaking havoc in my head. Constantine gave a moue of distaste when I suggested burgers, but he stopped at a drive-through and let me order.

"Let's pull over somewhere and at least pretend we're having a proper meal," he said when a paper bag full of fatty yumminess was safe on my lap.

I stuffed a handful of fries in my mouth and shrugged.

"You're so sexy like that," he said with a grin.

I tried to blow him a kiss, but the fries wouldn't allow it.

Laughing, he drove to an opening on the road, parked, and got out of the car.

"Where are you going?" I asked.

In lieu of an answer, he pulled a blanket out of the back seat and unfolded it on a grassy spot. He lay on his side and motioned for me to join him. I sat cross legged and placed the food strategically between us. Horizontal Constantine could lead to badness.

The carton-made barrier didn't help. I watched as he wrapped his lips around the fries or bit into a burger like it was the finest delicacy. The man oozed seduction, and my body responded to it. I adjusted my position, to ease the throbbing between my legs. Didn't work. He licked his fingers slowly, and I groaned before I could stop myself.

I blinked, and I was on my back, Constantine covering my body with his.

"Constantine…" My voice was hoarse. Better that it didn't work. I couldn't choose between telling him to stop or to rip off my clothes and fuck me in plain view of anyone who drove by.

"I've been good, Cherry," he whispered in my ear.

My insides clenched at the memory of Alex's weight on top of me, before he tried to kill me. As if he felt it, Constantine propped himself up on his arms. His eyes were violet but clear. I wasn't afraid of him. Never could be.

He licked his lips. "You've made me *want* to be good, and I plan on keeping it up. I won't pressure you into my bed, and I'll accept your decision if you only come to me for the ritual. But I don't want you to confuse my passiveness for lack of desire."

A tiny shift of my hips, and the proof of his words dug into my thigh. If he kissed me again, I wouldn't stop him.

Spoiler—he didn't.

"I burn for you," he said. "You are the only sunshine I care to touch. Thoughts of you consume my days, and that little sound you just made haunts my dreams. I said I won't be your default choice, and I meant it, but you should know it's sheer torture being this close and not touching you." He raised his hand to my face, let his fingers hover over my cheek for a brief moment, and then formed a fist and punched the ground next to my head.

I was at a loss. My skin hummed in response to his voice, as my brain scrambled to catch up with everything he said.

Constantine rolled off me and sat up. "I don't remember the last time I ate al fresco," he said in a pleasant, conversational tone. His eyes were their usual gorgeous blue again. He'd said his piece and left me in turmoil.

While I'd once blamed sensory memory for my response to his advances, I could no longer deny I wanted him. This was bad. So very bad. It was too soon after Alex to start something new, and the situation would be messy even without Alex in the picture. I couldn't get back together with Constantine, when I was about to give up my immortality.

I dug into my food, avoiding his gaze.

Fuck.

Chapter Four

Female voices reached me as we entered the mansion. The vampettes were used to their new reality—and they didn't have to travel the world for it. I mentally thanked whatever deity sent them to disrupt the tension between Constantine and me.

"I'll take my stuff to my room, and then come help with the move," I said.

Constantine nodded and went straight to the kitchen, while I made my way downstairs. I wasn't over what he'd said. Had he made a bet with himself to drive me nuts, with his *I love you too* and his declarations during our sort-of-a-picnic?

A quick shower washed away road dirt as well as thoughts I shouldn't be entertaining. I'd just put on my underwear and a fresh T-shirt, when Sheena barged in without knocking. My manager-turned-friend-turned-betrayer-turned-friend-again was more hyper than usual, as she hopped on my bed and bounced on her knees.

"Come on, come on, come on," she squealed.

"Someone's excited," I said as grumpily as I could, but I went closer for a hug. In truth, her excitement was refreshing. She'd lived in fear of Willoughby since my turning, and though she never showed weakness, this was the most carefree I'd seen her.

"I sure am," she said. "You're back, and the move is postponed for tomorrow. That means I don't have to carry shit *and* I get to drink."

"Yeah, 'cause you only drink on special days."

"God, I missed you." She laughed and squeezed me before letting go. "Tonight is girls' night in. The vampettes are making drinks, and your presence is mandatory." She hopped to her feet and tossed me my jeans. "Get dressed. The party is their room."

Their room. The one they shared with Constantine. Any lingering heat dissipated.

For a while, I'd done a great job convincing myself there was nothing sexual between my ex and his three protégés—though, let's face it, a man not known for his restraint shared his admittedly humongous bed with three sexy kittens. They sure as hell didn't play Sudoku when the door was closed.

I stretched and pulled my jeans back on. Immortality was supposed to keep me in a good shape, but I felt ancient. Because that was what emotional roller-coasters did to me.

What Constantine and his secrets and his stupid confessions of love did to me.

Love. *Pfft.* He meant it, but the word had a different meaning for him. I had to remember it when I considered giving us another chance. When we were together, he'd tried to convince me monogamy wasn't for vampires, and that sex and love were two distinct things. When I'd strongly disagreed, he'd cheated on me with his maker, and when I busted them, he insisted it was okay because he didn't have feelings for her.

Even if I accepted that immortals couldn't do physical fidelity, the lie was unforgivable. It'd be different if I'd agreed to an open relationship. Or a polyamorous one. I could maybe see myself with him and Alex.

I could totally see myself with him and Alex. In this bed. Or on the floor. They'd look so great naked together, Alex's tan contrasted against Constantine's pallor. Could I have them both? At the same time? It would be awkward after, but we could figure things out. And they both loved me. Well, Alex used to. I wasn't sure now.

Wait. Was I consideri—

"Earth to Cherry. Come in, Cherry." Sheena's voice snapped me out of it. She watched me, eyebrows furrowed. "Do I want to know what's in that head of yours?" she asked.

I shook said head.

"That's what I thought. Now button those up and let's go. Momma needs alcohol."

I followed her out of my room. Had I been thinking hard? Did I project my threesome-y thoughts to Constantine?

Speak of the devil… He stood outside his bedroom, tapping something on his phone. There was no sly look of *gotcha* in his eyes when we approached. He barely looked at me, as he said, "Alex called from the airport. He's on his way to London. I texted Ruby, and she and her team will pick him up at Heathrow."

"Did you tell him anything?" About the ritual.

Constantine shook his head. "I thought he should hear it from you."

"He didn't ask for me?" I kept my tone and face impassive, but I must have broadcasted my insecurity. Alex left to find himself. Maybe he also found that he no longer loved me.

And what the hell did I want?

Constantine snorted. "He was about to board. He'll call when he's with Ruby, and you can talk his ear off."

I rolled my eyes and shouldered past him and into the room. "Where's the music?" I asked. "I was promised a party."

"*Hey.*" Sally tackle-hugged me. She wasn't drunk, just naturally perky and friendly. Except for when she thought I meant to stake her. Or last time we spoke, when she was locked inside this room, crying and threatening to starve herself to dust, because she no longer wanted to be a vampire.

Constantine had talked her off the metaphorical ledge, and I'd stopped pretending he wasn't sleeping with her. With all of them. In the bed now covered with giggling girls, platters of snacks, and teetering glasses of margaritas.

I couldn't believe he let them endanger his precious silken sheets.

Sheena nudged me with her hip. "Grab a glass and tell us all about the big fight," she said. "Tall, blond, and dangerous said it's your story to share, and you only gave me the highlights over the phone."

I looked over my shoulder at Constantine, who winked. *"This is girls' night,"* he said inside my head. *"I'll wait it out upstairs, with my best whiskey."*

"Enjoy," I called after him and climbed on the bed. Vampires couldn't drink themselves to oblivion, but I'd give it a solid try.

Liza, unofficial leader of the three fledglings, turned down the music and crawled on the bed to join her two BFFs and Sheena, who sat cross legged in a semi-circle, facing me.

"So?" Sheena said.

"So you know the uber-bitch and her minion were haunting Alex, yes? They lied to him, built on his jealousy, and messed with his mind until he was barely himself." I stuffed a handful of nachos in my mouth and licked some salsa off my lips. "Well, the last night, they convinced him draining me was the only way to keep me from getting back together with Constantine."

"And he believed them?" Sheena asked. "He should have seen how broken you were when you thought he was dead. That boy needs an ass-whopping."

Nods all around.

The next part was hard to remember. Harder to put into words. So I tried to be as detached as possible and present things like an outside observer would. "He dragged me to the forest while I was trapped inside his dream. I woke to his fangs in my neck. My strength had fled and I knew I was almost gone."

Sally gasped. "He did that to you? But he loved you."

"He didn't realize he was killing me. When he did, he stopped. And then Willoughby attacked us." I shook my head, hoping to wipe away the memory of feeling helpless. I wasn't helpless. I won. Willoughby was dead.

"Where was Constantine?" Liza asked.

"Willoughby had staked him to the wall of my parents' basement"—insert collective gasp—"but he freed himself and came to the rescue. He fed me and then helped Alex."

Insert collective swoon. Yeah, yeah. Constantine was awesome.

"There was a fight, and Willoughby staked Alex but missed his heart. Alex pried out the stake and tossed it to me while Willoughby had Constantine pinned on the ground. I still can't believe I hit Willoughby's heart from where I lay half drained." I studied the girls for signs of discomfort. Willoughby had been their maker and was good to them… with the exception of killing them and wanting to turn them into undead assassins.

Carrie sighed. "We felt it when he was gone. We didn't know what we were feeling, but there was a snapping inside. A tearing, and then—"

"Hollowness," I said. I'd felt the same.

"It only lasted for a split second," Liza said. "We knew something big happened, but not what."

"Now you do," I said with a smile that hurt my cheeks. "Sorry I didn't have a more cheerful story for you."

Liza waved off my concern, and Sheena patted my knee. "Alex will be back," she said. "He loves you."

"I know. And he had a good reason for going away." And maybe one day I'd believe that.

"Why did he leave?" the third vampette, Carrie, asked.

Lovely. I had to explain something I barely understood. "He felt bad for attacking me"—for almost perma-killing me—"and he needed some distance to figure out how to fix things. He thought helping out more of the fledglings Willoughby and Ádísa created would be a good step in that direction." Or something.

"So to make up for what he did to you, he left you behind and went to help girls he'd never met?" The scowl was out of place on Sally's lovely face. Especially when she twirled a blond curl around her fingers.

"That makes no sense," Liza added. Her dark eyebrows were pulled together too, shadowing her hazel eyes. "Why not stay and fix things? I appreciate his altruism—got us out of a potentially shitty situation—but it does jack shit for *you*."

"He said he hadn't come to terms with being a vampire. That he wasn't himself since he was turned. He wanted to do good on a larger scale, to feel better, and then come to me in equal terms," I said.

Carrie harrumphed. She was the most level headed of the three, balancing between Liza's quick temper and Sally's naiveté. "What equal terms? He'll still be the jackass who hurt you out of jealousy. He attacked you, Cherry. If you were both humans, he'd be arrested for it."

Or I'd be dead.

"No," I said. Another sip of strawberry-laced tequila might help. "He'll prove to himself he can still be *Alex*, so then he'll know he won't hurt me again." His aggression had horrified me, but I knew it wasn't him. My mind and heart trusted him. In time, my body would learn to do so again too. But he had to be here for that to happen. Instead, he ran away, and I was left defending a decision I didn't agree with.

Liza cupped my shoulder. "But will *you* know?"

Constantine chose that moment to knock on the open door. "You better wrap this up, children. We have a busy day tomorrow."

I was so grateful for the interruption, I didn't care how much he'd heard.

Chapter Five

We moved Sheena and the girls out the next afternoon. It was fun, except for the carrying-stuff-around-while-pretending-to-be-humans thing, and Sheena totally enjoyed ordering us around until the rooms she provided the vampettes were to her liking. We ate and had a drink or two, and then, as much as I delayed the inevitable, Constantine and I had to return to the mansion.

Alone.

My ass buzzed the moment it touched the passenger's seat. I pulled my phone out of my pocket and let out a sigh of relief. Alex. *And* I didn't have to make chitchat with Constantine.

"Hey, you," I said.

Constantine looked at me, and I mouthed *Alex*. He started the car, but we didn't move. So much for this phone call saving us some awkwardness.

"Hey." Alex's voice was warm and sexy as ever. "Wanted to let you know I landed safely."

I glanced at the dashboard clock. "A couple hours ago." Which I hadn't noticed till now. Shame on me.

"I'm sorry. Ruby picked me up at the airport, and we had a bite to eat before driving to the hotel she's staying at. We started talking, and I lost track of time. She's a fascinating lady."

I shouldn't be jealous of my grandma, who really was fascinating. And kickass. And looked like she could be my slightly older sister. And I wouldn't be jealous of her.

"So will you be staying in London," I asked?

"I thought so at first, but Ruby has a plan. We'll be doing recon—fly to a different European city every couple days, verify the location of the fledglings' to be rehabilitated, and make first contact. With Willoughby and Ádísa out of the picture, they may be easier to approach."

"Or they may be panicking."

That was what he wanted to talk about? No *I miss you*?

"That's a possibility too, and we're ready for it. Ruby has made connections with a couple European Masters who'll help us."

It took me a moment to catch up. European vampires have a different social structure. Each area has its own Master, whose word is law for his jurisdiction.

"Please stay safe," I said.

"I will. Honest. I want to get back home in one piece."

He could have said *to you*. He didn't. Should I be reading things into this? "Good. When you have time, there's something else we need to discuss."

"We have a few more seconds. Ruby doesn't want me on this phone longer than that. I'll get a burner phone tomorrow and text you the number."

So very *Cloak and Dagger*. Was there even an enemy they were hiding from, or was this all so our council wouldn't find Ruby? "It's not urgent, and I'd rather do it over video-chat," I told him.

He chuckled. "It may be a while for that. Ruby doesn't trust any online connection but her own, and we won't be in her camp for at least another two weeks."

"I'll wait."

Silence for a second, then— "I'm happy to hear that. I'll call you from the new phone, okay?"

"Okay."

"Love you."

He hadn't said it since he left, and he hung up now before I could say the same. Might be for the best. Even if I had it in me to voice the words, I didn't wanna do so in front of Constantine.

"All good?" Constantine asked.

"Yup. Ruby will drag him all around Europe."

He shook his head. "That woman always has a purpose."

"Yeah." Now what to talk about?

"Wanna go home, get drunk, and fuck like animals?"

I snapped my head toward him and saw his body shake with suppressed laughter. I smacked his leg. "What would you do if I said *yes*?"

Mirth disappearing, he grabbed my wrist and led my hand higher on his thigh. "Say it and see."

Thus began two very torturous weeks.

I don't know if Constantine did it on purpose, but he made it impossible for me to avoid him around the mansion. Every time I left my room, he was there, topless more often than not, and always with that sexy I-know-you-want me smirk.

Despite his obvious availability, our exchanges were polite, bordering on stilted.

Have you fed?

Did you hear from Alex?

Do you need something?

Sheena and the girls are settling in well.

Here are your council bank account details and a credit card.

Let's go over the prophecy again.

The last one never yielded new results. We had to have sex and be sucked near-dry while climaxing. He was convinced forcing Alex's blood through my lips when I was near perma-death would spare Constantine and rehumanize me. And probably Alex too. There was no recorded case of vampires trying this before, but Constantine believed if I turned human again, so would the only vampire I made— Alex. There were no guarantees. At least Constantine wasn't in danger of dusting. Worst case scenario, it didn't work.

Wesley was pulling a vanishing act and only showed his face to bring coffee or reheated blood with Ruby's brew. With the other human and the vampettes out of the mansion, he didn't need to prepare meals for us, and he spent his free time in his rooms or visiting Sheena. He reportedly was teaching her to cook.

To add to the discomfort of my new reality, since Alex's self-actualization journey teamed him up with my grandma, all I heard from him was, *Ruby is so cool* and *Ruby knows what to do* and *You should hear Ruby's rendition of Any-Song-Ever*.

He didn't say those three little words again, but I didn't mind. It made it easier for me to function without constantly wondering about the mess that was our relationship. If there still was such a thing.

The morning before we were supposed to talk on Skype, I couldn't sleep. I tossed and turned, wondering how he'd take the news. Wondering why I cared. *He* left *me*. Now we had a chance for a real life. *I* had a chance for a real life, with or without him. If Alex couldn't push aside his ego and give it a try, Constantine and I would have to find someone else for me to feed on during the ritual.

If I went ahead with the ritual.

I had to put on my big-girl pants and talk to Constantine.

No time like the present.

Fresh out of big-girl pants, I pulled on a pair of sweats and dragged my feet to his door. There'd be time to sort things out after we talked to Alex, but I had to know

now—if I became human again, would Constantine have a place in my life? Would he want one?

I tapped my fingertips on his bedroom door. It wasn't two seconds, before his voice in my head said, *"Come in, Cherry."*

I turned the handle and pushed, praying he was dressed or covered, so I could stay focused.

He was propped up in bed, blood-red satin sheets mercifully covering him well above his waist. He was still breathtaking, with his long golden hair draping his muscular shoulders and his angular face cast in the soft glow of candles.

His expression wasn't seductive, though. It was concerned. And I was thankful for it.

"Are you all right?" he said aloud. "Is something the matter?"

"I just want to talk. Is that okay?"

"Of course." He sat up higher, and I was relieved to see the waist of his PJ bottoms peek out from under the sheets. He patted the mattress next to him. How convenient that there was nowhere else to sit in the whole room. He sensed my reluctance, because he said, "No funny business."

I climbed on the humongous bed and sat cross-legged, facing him.

"Is this about Alex?" he asked through our mental link.

"Yes and no." I still felt weird, thinking things at him, so I didn't.

"Tell me," he said with a sigh.

"You really believe the ritual's going to make me human? Alex too?"

A shadow darkened his blue eyes, and he averted his gaze. "I do."

"And it'll keep you safe?"

"It'll keep me from dusting."

Not the same. "But you'll be affected in some way?"

His smile and eyes were brilliant when he looked at me again. "Undoubtedly. The mere thought affects me." He glided his palm down his thigh, and I saw the outline of his erection under the thin fabric of his sheets.

I set my jaw before I did something stupid, like bite my lip and moan. When I regained control of myself, I said, "A *breeze* affects that." We had this exchange before, but it held true. The man was a horndog. "I'm talking about actual physical harm. Will the ritual cause you any?"

"No. I'll remain my devastatingly handsome self long after he's old and senile and can't get it up."

I stared at my hands, folded in my lap. "And if it works, what then?"

"You and Alex get your happily-ever-after, I guess." He sounded like a different man to the one who days ago said he burned for me.

"What will happen to *us*? You and me? Will I still see you?"

He got to his knees and leaned closer. "Why would you want to? You'll get back the life that was stolen from you. You'll build a family with the man you love. Why should I be a part of that?"

I started to say because he was my friend, but it wasn't what he wanted to hear. And it was a lie.

He grabbed my wrists, and I looked up at the storm in his eyes. "If you ask me to be in your life, I will," he whispered, "and it will hurt me with every breath you take. Every time your heart beats, I'll be reminded... Spare me and let me go, Cherry. You've obviously made your decision. Don't make mine for me."

I wanted to scream that this wasn't fair; he'd made decisions for me before. I opened my mouth, but what came out was, "But I love you."

"Then choose me." The hope and yearning in his voice closed like an iron fist around my unbeating heart.

It would mean remaining a vampire. Giving up on normalcy for good. Giving up on Alex.

Did I want Alex back? Shouldn't I have the chance to find out? I knew I loved Constantine the moment I uttered it, but I also loved Alex. Could I be with either of them, after how both relationships ended?

I needed more data, damn it, but one thing was certain.

"I can't," I muttered. I resented my vampire nature for years; I had to give being human again a shot. If I chose Constantine now, I might end up hating him.

He let go, and I felt bereft. "I could erase your memory when you're human," he said. "Make you forget all about us. You might be happier that way."

"No." Out of the question. My past was part of who I was, and nobody tampered with it. Funny how I once thought taking away Alex's memories of me was a good idea.

Constantine nodded. "It might be safer for you to move to Europe, to make sure the council doesn't catch wind of your new situation. Alternatively, you could stage a semi-public staking or walk in the sun and stay here, incognito. Even so, I'd move to a different state. You'll have to find a place. Maybe a job—though I know someone who can funnel money from your council funds into an untraceable account."

My gut twisted at the thought of leaving everything behind. Or maybe it was because of how detached Constantine sounded. As if we'd already said *goodbye*. "I'll stay in L.A.," I said. "I respect that you don't want to see me after, but I'm not starting over again. I'll talk to Sheena. See if I can help her with the agency. I'll find an apartment."

"So your decision is final?"

Was it? Doubt threatened to choke me. "Maybe. No. I'll let you know when it is."

He surprised me by sliding back under the covers and folding one corner back for me. "It's late," he said. "Let's get some sleep."

I slipped in next to him, and he gathered me close, my head on his chest. "I missed this," I murmured, splaying my palm over his bare stomach. I ran my fingertips over the soft down beneath his navel. I was playing with fire, and part of me hoped I'd get burned. That he'd suck me back into the vortex that was loving him, and make me forget my need to see what could be. That he'd fuck me into oblivion and delete all other options from my mind.

He didn't. He tangled his fingers with mine and brought our joined hands to his chest. *"I want nothing more than to bury myself inside you, but I won't be a diversion,"* he said in my head.

Infuriating man.

He held me until I fell asleep, and then he joined me in my dream and lay beside me on the beach till late in the evening.

When we were to talk to Alex.

Chapter Six

"Cherry, can't you see he's lying through his teeth? I can, and I'm in a different continent." Alex shook his head, the motion pixelated by his crappy internet connection. He didn't sound half as upset as he'd have been a month ago. "This is desperate, Cee. What happened to not being the default choice?"

I sighed. "As fucked up as it sounds, I don't think he made up the prophecy. Let him explain."

Constantine sat back in his chair, arms folded over his chest, looking from me to the screen.

"Aren't you gonna say something?" I asked him. Under the harsh artificial lighting, the intimacy we shared earlier was replaced by our usual snarky banter.

"Anything I say at this point will be held against me." A smile curved his full lips. "Besides, this is fun."

"See? He's messing with your head, so you sleep with him."

But I already slept with him, and he made no move to take what was obviously on offer. "There are easier ways to go about that," I said.

"Nice." Alex scowled, but his voice held no anger. It was a refreshing change from the growly, jealous, and ultimately dangerous side of him Ádísa and Willoughby had spent months bringing to the surface. "If vampires could become human again, Ruby would have told me."

Because they were so close. Ugh.

"She told *me*," Constantine said, before I came up with a snarky response. "You've known her for all of a fortnight. I'm her maker. Besides, I happened upon part of the scripture several centuries ago, and Ruby knew that when she discovered the translation." His flared nostrils were the only indication of his annoyance.

What Constantine didn't say was that Ruby didn't want Alex to know. The prophecy was about vampires who'd killed their makers, and Alex's maker was yours truly. If he was determined to become human again, I might be at risk. Constantine convinced her there was no chance Alex would do something like that.

Alex leaned closer to the screen. "How come you're only now mentioning it?" Seeing him in detective mode was familiar. Soothing.

"I didn't know what it meant till Ruby filled in the gaps," Constantine said. "I'm still not entirely certain—"

"I *knew* it. You're working an angle. I can't believe you're using Cherry's grandmother as a cover. She's literally a wall away. I can easily check your story. Good idea, poor execution. You should have gone for something vaguer, man. You're losing your touch."

So my latest ex was giving my previous ex advice on how to… *get in my pants*? "Both of you, shut up," I said, before that thought led me astray. "Constantine, take it from the top. Alex, please don't interrupt this time."

"I'll try." Alex sounded tired.

"Right. As I told Cherry, I was in the Varangian Guard in Byzantium, in the tenth century. Back then, it was called—"

I rolled my eyes. "Without the history lesson this time, please."

Constantine sucked in his cheeks, accentuating his cheekbones. After sleeping in his arms, I found shooing away lustful thoughts about him was harder than ever.

But my lack of a sex life wasn't the focus of this meeting, though it was heavily involved.

"Here is the condensed version, then, for those among us with the attention span of a coleopteron." Constantine smirked. "Our job was to protect the emperor. During the battle of—"

I faked a snore.

"During *a* battle, I was forced to spend the night in a monastery's catacombs. It was completely undignified, having to share a tomb with a freshly interred priest, but in his robes I found a torn parchment."

We'd analyzed the prophecy to death the past couple weeks, but Constantine hadn't mentioned his turning again, so I wasn't surprised he said nothing about it now.

"You searched a dead priest's robes?" Alex asked.

"I was trying to fashion some sort of headrest. I'd elaborate, but Cherry is in a hurry for me to finish the story."

"Yeah, go ahead." I crossed my legs and fiddled with my sneaker's shoelaces.

"Yes, please get to the part that says you and Cherry must have sex, for her to become human again," Alex said.

"I told you that wasn't the right way to preface it," Constantine said to me. "Anyway, at the time it made little sense but provided an opportunity for me to exercise my Greek. Now we have the complete text, the part that applies to us loosely translates to:

> *If two immortals who have shorn their own roots are consumed to the brink of death while taking each other, they can walk under the sun and count finite remaining sunsets once again, requiring breath and sustenance, and growing as nature and God meant Man to."*

"Either the prototype or the translation could be utter bull-crap," Alex said. "Cherry, he may not even speak Greek, for all we know."

"He kind of does," I said. He tried to teach me, years ago, but it didn't take.

"Fluently," Constantine supplied.

"Of course you do," Alex mumbled. "And according to your *fluent* translation, you two are supposed to fuck"—an edge flashed through his voice, before he reined it back in—"while draining each other."

"You can check with Ruby," I said with a sneer.

"We're two vampires who've killed their own makers. Shorn our own roots, in a way," Constantine said. "But there's no mention of draining each other. Only of being drained."

"And then you'll be human again?" Alex asked.

"Cherry will." Constantine shrugged. "I'll be dust. There's a short line about how we'll each revert to what we'd be in human years."

Alex raked the fingers of both hands through his hair. "Cee, if you're lying, you're better at it than I thought. Offering your unlife for a night with Cherry is kind of risky."

His half-assed attempt at a joke didn't make me laugh. "This is serious," I said. "But there may be a way out."

"Of course there is." Alex slapped his thigh. His video shook for a second, before his face came back into focus. "The man is my hero. Now he'll tell us about his brilliant plan that involves the two of you naked and him surviving the prophecy. And when you're still a vampire afterward, you'll have to forgive him, because—hey—he tried."

When Alex and I were together, he'd expressed his distrust of Constantine repeatedly and aggressively. Now he grinned and seemed to admire Constantine for the elaborate scheme he'd supposedly concocted.

Men are weird, but mine are extra wonky.

"Actually, my plan involves all three of us," Constantine said, and I went to my happy place before I could stop myself. "If I take and consume Cherry but she doesn't drain me, she may be the only one turned back."

"Or she dies from exsanguination." Alex's voice dropped to a whisper.

"That's where you come in," Constantine said. "The moment before I drain her completely, you force your blood down her throat."

"So I'll be in the room, while the two of you get it on."

"See the big picture," I said. "Assuming legend and Hollywood"—and Constantine—"have it right, if I turn human, so does my progeny. You get your life back. The council never found out about you, so you don't have to hide."

"You may even pick up a couple of tricks, if you watch closely." Constantine winked at the screen. "Should you feel so inclined, Cherry may finally get the ménage—"

I used my vampire speed to flip down the lid of the laptop. Not the way to end a Skype call, as I always yelled at the TV when actors did it, but it was all I could think of, to keep Alex from hearing the end of that sentence.

"—à trois she and Sheena have been talking about."

I wagged my finger at Constantine. "You weren't supposed to hear that. It was a private conversation."

My phone rang, and I groaned. *Alex.*

"Did he say you want a threesome?" he asked when I picked up.

Could a girl have no secrets?

"He's being a jerk," I said.

"But you believe him?"

"Yes."

"And you want to go through with this?"

I sighed. "I don't know. I want to be human again. I think. It's a big decision."

"There's a flight from Bucharest to L.A. at ten in the morning, local time. If I make it, I'll be there early afternoon. We'll figure it out then."

I was more than a little relieved that Alex didn't press for more information on the threesome thing, but it didn't stop me from glaring at Constantine when I got off the phone.

"What? I was trying to get you your wish." He sounded happy with himself.

"I don't know if I wanna do this. And we were supposed to get Alex to consider it, not scare him away," I said.

"The prospect of sharing you with me may be daunting for your boyfriend, but I doubt he found it scary. He's trying to get back into your good graces. Why would he turn down an opportunity to join us in bed?"

"Because he might want me to himself? Because if he's my boyfriend—like you said—he won't share me, which you seem more than eager to."

"Cherry, I don't want your pussy to myself. I want *you*. I meant what I said about monogamy. After hundreds of years on this world, I don't consider it a prerequisite for a successful relationship."

"Still with that excuse?"

He held up a hand. "Regardless, I should have respected how much it means to you, and I wish I could make that right. But we're no longer together, Alex is a striking man, and the three of us can have an incredible time together before you and he ride off into the sunset."

If he put it this way… I rolled my shoulders and allowed myself two-point-five seconds of daydreaming. It would feel amazing, being pressed between two hard male bodies that defined beauty, but it'd be for a single night. Would having a taste make me crave more?

Constantine stood and stretched, and I was grateful he'd put on a shirt for Alex's sake. I'd seen enough of him the past couple weeks, and I still felt his naked chest against my cheek.

"So you wouldn't mind me sleeping with someone else while we were together?" I asked.

"*Sleeping with*, I'd mind. Fucking, no. I could watch, or you could tell me every sordid detail afterward, while I ravaged you."

Though the idea made me wet, he, Alex, and I had achieved a fragile balance. The ritual could throw a wrench into things. What if having Constantine inside me again made me realize I didn't want to give him up? What if Alex saw the connection I shared with my ex and fled? What if I ended up more confused than I was now *and* with no options?

And Constantine had lost his shirt again.

"Will you stop undressing, while we're talking serious stuff?" I asked. *One. Two. Three. Four...* Had to stop counting abs, but—yup. Six. All there.

He smirked and flexed his pecs. "I thought we were done talking. Alex is flying in tomorrow, and you'll have to make up your mind. Then you and Mr. Marsden can be on your merry way, to have offspring and frolic in the sun, while I return to the debauchery a single male vampire of my stature is supposed to indulge in." Pretentious, run-on sentences were another defense of his, and he used them well, but his tricks didn't work on me.

Until he leaned over me and planted his large palms on the back of my chair. "So unless there's something more you need..."

I was trapped between his arms, having no choice but to look at his chest or straight into his eyes. Violet flecked their usual blue.

Violet meant lust. A hunger I ached to sate but needed to steer clear from.

"Nope. Nothing more for now," I told his chest. Believe it or not, staring at that was the safe choice.

"Good." *Liar.* Regret laced the single word as he straightened and walked toward the stairs leading to the basement.

It would be easy to run after him, tackle him on his bed, and ride him to oblivion, but even if going down that path didn't lead to heartache this time, I had Alex to consider.

My noble Alex, half the world away from L.A. His reactions to our conversation earlier showed he'd done a lot of growing. He was getting used to his new nature, and he had control over his emotions and jealousy.

And Constantine and I were finally at a good place. In retrospect, I was begrudgingly grateful he didn't make a move when I was all over him this morning. We were open about our feelings and enjoying each other's company. Except for the awkward silences and the times I wanted to shred the clothes off him and lick—

What the hell was I doing?

I was faced with the biggest dilemma ever and wasted mental energy on things that didn't matter. I let my feelings for Constantine and my uncertainty about Alex spin me in circles. I should decide whether or not to go through with the ritual based on the future I wanted, not on which guy I was more into right now.

I ought to do some soul searching of my own. Maybe help other people, like Alex and my grandma did.

After I helped myself to some blood.

I headed downstairs. The mini fridge in the basement was always stocked with blood, and I could call Sheena from my room. She was practical; she'd be a good sounding board.

Chapter Seven

"Do it." Sheena's voice brooked no argument.

"You realize it'll be a new beginning? In all ways?" I didn't consent to my turning, but I hadn't been human in ages. "I can't pick up where I left off. And I'll be thirty, not a frozen-in-time twenty-four."

"Listen, hon. Everything you've told me shows your mind is made up. I know it, you know it, and Tall-Blond-and-Deadly knows it. You told him you can't choose him. We're beating a dead horse."

"You're right, I guess." So was I trying to make sure I made the right choice, or to talk myself out of it?

"Do it," she said again. "If only for the crazy sexytimes. You'll live the fantasy of anyone who's ever laid eyes on those boys. We'll get you a job. And you can stay with me till you find a new place if you don't wanna shack up with Alex. The girls are used to sharing their space, so I've got a spare room."

"But—"

"Stop over thinking it, Cherry. You never wanted to be a vampire. This is your chance. Go for it, and maybe record the ritual, for those less fortunate than you?"

"You're an idiot." But I was chuckling. "And the sex part scares me too. I'm not crazy about the idea of Alex watching me with Constantine."

Sheena harrumphed. "If he's only watching, you're doing it wrong. Give the man a side and let him play."

"A side?"

"Yeah. Does he get in the front or the back? Decide who goes where, and then relax and enjoy it."

"*Sheena.*" I pulled off sounding shocked, while my mind juxtapositioned visuals with different combinations of the three of us. Some didn't have me in the middle.

"Right. I forgot your delicate sensibilities, Ms. I-Wanna-be-a-Porn-Star. This is a one-time thing, correct?"

"Yes." A potentially incredible one-time thing…

"Then why are we having this discussion?"

I didn't know. Not like it was helping me make up my mind. "So you don't think me becoming mortal again is a bad idea?" I asked.

"Hell, no. And if you hate it, you can always go back."

As if.

I spent my vampire years bemoaning the things I'd never do. Now I could do them. I'd stop self-sabotaging and get on with it. Whoever wanted to stick around afterward was more than welcome.

I thanked Sheena for hearing me out and ended the call with a promise to visit as soon as possible. I wanted *everything* to happen as soon as possible. I couldn't take the next step till Alex was here, but I could let Constantine know my decision was final.

"I'll do it," I said, barging into his room.

He wasn't there. Better. He tended to be naked in his room, and I had to stay the course. I flew up the stairs and found him reading the paper in the kitchen, two cups of steaming blood on the table in front of him.

"Sit. Drink," he said.

"I wanna become human again," I blurted and dropped on the chair to his right. "I'm certain."

He rolled the paper and tapped it on the kitchen table, like a makeshift drumstick. "I was hoping you'd change your mind. This world is going to hell. Humans kill each other over imaginary infractions. Politics and religion divide communities and turn the masses into rabid zealots. The people refuse to learn from the past, and humanity is constantly on the brink of several wars. And you want to revert to being one of them."

He let go of the paper and grasped the table with both hands. "You will lose your immortality. Things will be able to hurt you. No superhuman strength. You won't fly or see the colors come to life after sundown. You will no longer have the connection to the world that vampires do. Are you ready for these losses?"

They didn't matter. *He* did, and I was as ready to lose him as I'd ever be—not at all. "But I'll hear my heart beat again, Constantine. I'll be able to have a family. Mortality comes with an expiration date, and that makes life more… *more*."

He clenched his jaw and squeezed his eyes shut. I watched his knuckles whiten with tension. He wasn't getting this.

"When you know you may not be around tomorrow, you seek out experiences. Take risks. Feel things," I said.

Constantine flipped the table straight across the room. It crashed into the fridge, leaving both in shambles. "Vampires fucking *feel* things, Cherry," he roared. When he looked at me, pain swirled in his eyes. "*I* fucking feel things. *You* fucking feel things. You want me as much as I want you. I see it. I feel it in my skin. Your heart doesn't beat, but you love me. This isn't about feeling. This is about doing what you've been taught is right. You don't even want a family, but you'll be a good little girl and force yourself to fit a mold you broke long ago. So I'll fuck the immortality out of you, and then I don't want to see you again."

He stomped out of the kitchen, leaving me plenty of time to stop him. I didn't. Constantine was always composed except for the glimpses of sentiment he allowed me at his most vulnerable or honest moments. His eruption shocked me. And though it didn't scare me—he'd never hurt me—his words landed on me like punches.

I wasn't doing this to fit a mold. I wanted to be human. I'd reclaim all that was stolen from me. I'd be happy.

And if Constantine didn't get that, maybe it was best that we never saw each other again afterward.

A huge crack ran along the table's surface, where the impact splintered the wood. The door of the fridge had snapped inward, creating an opening for fruit and blood bags to spill to the floor. The two mugs had shattered against the wall and the floor, their contents making the room look like a crime scene.

Wesley would have someone clean up, and all that was broken would be replaced by morning. But I'd seen the damage, and it would stay with me.

* * * *

Bagged blood wouldn't cut it, after all. I was feeling antsy and didn't want to run into Constantine again. I could go by Sheena's, but I wasn't in the mood for company either. If Alex got on board, this might be my last night as a vampire, and I'd spend it hunting.

The chill in the air was refreshing against my cool skin. I let my eyes adjust and took in the vibrant hues the night brought to life. Constantine was right; I'd miss this. But not enough. I once felt sorry for Alex, because his world was so different to mine. I turned him soon after, to save him from death. Now I could give him his world back and me with it. Vamp-sight was a small price to pay.

I took off for downtown, loving the rush lift-off shot through my veins. I didn't like my donors intoxicated, but a little alcohol in their system gave me a light buzz while I fed, and that was more than welcome tonight.

I got my wish and my fill from a frat boy who was enjoying his friend's drunken misery a little too much. The punk was recording, while the other guy puked his guts out and cried for the boy who broke his heart. I fed on the first one, deleted the video on his phone, and then thralled him to have the world's worst hangover in the morning. Then I turned my vampire gaze to his heartbroken buddy, sobered him up, and sent him to shower. All in a good day's work, huh?

The sun was almost up when I returned to the mansion. I tiptoed inside and was glad to be greeted by darkness and quiet. If Constantine was home, he wasn't on the ground floor. I didn't see him on the way to my room and heard no sign of him while I got ready for bed. Good. We had more than our share of emotional moments this week.

I was in bed when I heard the front door open and shut again. I kept my eyes closed and listened to Constantine's footsteps cross the living room above me and then descend the stairs to the basement. They stopped outside my door. "Are you awake?"

I wasn't sure if the question was out loud or in my head, but I considered ignoring it either way. *Nah.* "Come in."

He opened the door, and I rolled on my side, to face him. He leaned on the doorframe and folded his arms over his wide chest. "I'm sorry for my outburst earlier."

Outburst was an understatement, but apologizing doesn't come naturally to Constantine, and I appreciated the effort. "It's okay. Your kitchen, your mess."

"That mess is fixed. It's what's between us I hope to mend. I shouldn't have reacted that way. I asked Ruby to let me be the one to tell you about the prophecy because I wanted to make you happy. My actions don't show that. I don't wish to see you when you're human, because I can't watch you die with every day that passes. It's not a punishment for you; it's a way to safeguard me from more sorrow. That said, I'll never turn my back to you. If you need me, I'll be there. I'll cover for you with the council. And I'll love you till the day I dust."

Not a single word could make it past the knot in my throat. I nodded and thought at him, *"Thank you."*

Saying I loved him again would get us nowhere.

Chapter Eight

Constantine offered to pick up Alex at the airport, but Alex said he'd get a cab. Good idea. Safe.

Didn't keep me from pacing the living room from the moment Alex texted he landed in L.A. to when the intercom buzzed for Wesley to let him in the gate.

I threw the front door open, but trepidation trumped excitement when Alex got out of the taxi and ducked back in for his duffel bag. Would reverting to his mortal self write out what he did as a vampire, in my mind or his?

He looked good as ever, his jeans hugging his toned ass and legs, and his polo shirt straining to contain his muscular back and arms. Yummy.

But was I allowed to enjoy the yumminess?

He said he loved me two weeks ago, but not since. He obviously cared, or he wouldn't have hopped on a plane back when I told him about the prophecy. Though maybe he did that because he wanted to become human again.

And how did I feel about the prospect of him touching me? I used to enjoy his touch, but then he'd hurt me. Would my body remember how he made it arch with pleasure, or cling to the terror of his fangs buried in my neck when he almost dusted me?

My smile hurt my face. Did it look fake? Should I hug him? Kiss him?

He saved me from myself by wrapping both arms around me and planting a kiss at the corner of my mouth. "You're a sight for sore eyes."

So he was into me and his proximity didn't make me balk. No panic rushed in. Yay! I held on, enjoying his hard body against mine. "Hey, you. Long time no see," I said.

He let go and offered his hand to Constantine, who came up behind me.

Constantine pulled him in for that half-hug, half-pat-on-the-back thing men do. "Welcome home, Alex."

Home. Not for long. Alex still had his place in the city. I might move in with him.

One step at a time. My new motto.

I tugged him inside the mansion. "Come. Take a nap, and when you wake up, you can tell us everything."

"Want some blood first?" Constantine asked.

"Yeah. I'm starving."

Wesley was already brewing his miracle coffee that could keep vampires awake in mid-day.

"I'll have a cup of that," I said.

"Which I'll pour," Constantine said. He turned to the aging human. "Get some rest, Wesley. We're good here."

"If you say so, sir." Wesley gave a tiny bow and left us.

The three of us.

Alone.

Together.

Did I hammer that point home yet?

No? Let me try again.

I was alone in the kitchen with two men I was incredibly drawn to—whom I loved—and we had to discuss the possibility of me having sex with one while the other watched, so I could cut all ties to the former and maybe spend my human years with the latter.

Just your usual Tuesday.

Alex sank into one of the new kitchen chairs that came with the new kitchen table and looked around. "Did you redecorate?"

I looked at Constantine, who was reheating the blood. He shrugged.

"So how was Europe? How were things with Ruby? Did you locate any of Willoughby's fledglings?" I asked, while Constantine placed a mug of blood in front of Alex and handed me my coffee.

"Ruby is amazing." Alex beamed. "She's on top of everything. All her leads were good. We found six more women, and Ruby and her team will rehabilitate them. Things are different in Europe. The local Masters were getting restless with new vampires entering their turfs, so they were on Willoughby's trail too. Seems he and Ádísa started over there, to stay under the U.S. council's radar. Their European childer"—that's the plural for *childe*, by the way—"awaited orders for the next step of the plan." To take over the world, using top-model vampire mercenaries. *That* plan. "Most of them weren't happy with the change in regime. Convincing them their makers were the bad guys will take a lot of work, but if anyone can do it—"

It'd be Ruby.

"—it's Ruby."

Cause she was amazing. Ugh.

"Your turn," Alex said to Constantine. "Is the prophecy real?"

Constantine leaned against the counter and crossed his arms. "To the best of my knowledge."

"And if you do the ritual as is, will it kill you?"

"Yes."

Alex blew some air in his mug, then gulped down the contents. "But you'll do it anyway?"

"I don't have a death wish; I'd prefer another vampire to help us. If none will, then yes. I'll do it," Constantine said.

I believed him, and apparently so did Alex, because he said, "I can't let you make all the sacrifices. Doesn't look good for me."

"So you're in?" I asked.

"As long as we're clear on what that entails. Can I wait outside the room till you call me?"

"I'm afraid not," Constantine replied. "Timing is everything, and you'll have to be within reach."

Alex didn't seem pleased, but he said, "Okay. When?"

"When do you want?" I asked.

"The sooner, the better."

"How about midnight tonight?" asked Constantine.

Too soon. I still needed answers. Alex was back, but was he here to stay? And would we get back together? Should we?

One step at a time.

"Midnight it is," I said.

"My room," Constantine said.

Alex nodded and stood. "I'd like a shower and that nap now."

Soon he was in the downstairs bathroom, while I sat on the bed we used to share, listening to the water pelting his skin, while my thoughts wandered. He and I were thrown together by circumstance and bonded by danger. Once we were human again—*if* we were human again—could we have the relationship he wanted? Maybe someday a family?

We had hours till midnight when he emerged from the bathroom. We could fill them with chitchat or talk more about his trip and my forays into the dream-world.

"What happens when we're both human?" I asked instead. "Do we date? Give us a try?"

He studied my face. "Are you open to that? I thought you and Constantine… You smell like him."

Shit. Should have showered. "I slept in his bed, but there's nothing—" *Lie.* There *was* something between

Constantine and me. I shook my head. "Nothing happened. I was lonely and confused, and we talked till I fell asleep."

"You still have feelings for him."

After tonight, they wouldn't matter. I could lie now, and Alex would never be the wiser. I didn't. "I always will, like I'll always have feelings for you. But I won't stay with him, and I'm asking if you want us to be something."

I felt like a hypocrite. I wasn't choosing Alex; I was choosing mortality. If the choice were between him and Constantine... No way to know.

"So you forgive me for what I did to you?" he asked.

I did. I had. But could I forget it? Not trusting myself to speak, I nodded.

A timid smile blossomed on his lips. "I want us to be *everything*. I want to have a future with you. To grow old with you."

I couldn't tell if I was elated or suffocated; my head was light, and my feet felt made of lead.

Alex crossed the distance between us and laid a gentle kiss on my lips. "Tomorrow on, when I do this, I'll be able to feel your heartbeat," he said. His palm was on my chest, but there was nothing sexual about the touch.

I let him pull me into his gleeful ramblings. We'd redecorate his apartment. Maybe get a dog. I'd get a job, possibly with Sheena, and he'd see if he could return to the force. We could go somewhere exotic next summer—we earned a sunny vacation, after the crap we dealt with. And his mom would be ecstatic if he told her we were engaged.

What?

"We can pick out a ring together. Anything you want." Alex took my hand and brushed his thumb over my ring finger.

"A ring?" *What what what?*

"I don't mean now. We'll see how things go. But I'll make you happy, Cherry." A shadow crossed his eyes, and he added, "I'll never hurt you again. I swear."

I squeezed his fingers and leaned in closer, my face inches from his. "I know." If we were kissing, we didn't have to talk, and I didn't have to think of how a few weeks of chasing hot women alongside my grandma had freed him from the guilt of almost killing me for good.

Alex crushed his mouth to mine and nibbled on my lower lip before thrusting his tongue between my lips, to find mine. While demanding, his kiss wasn't threatening. I felt bad for allowing memories of a past he couldn't control interfere with this moment. The darkness had washed out of him, and he was my Alex again, now and forever.

Funny how long *forever* sounded when our future was finite.

Chapter Nine

I was surprised when Constantine got the door for us instead of bidding us enter, but then I realized it was to show off how gorgeous he looked in his robe. Sashed around his waist, it accentuated his wide shoulders and narrow waist, and allowed glimpses of his chest. The dark-purple silk made his pallor luminescent.

He was barefoot, and his hair was pulled back in a—

"Is that a man-bun?" I asked.

He flashed a smile. "Carrie showed me an instructional video. The abundance of positive comments convinced me to give it a try."

I wanted to say something snarky, but the updo enhanced his savage beauty. *Shit.* Shouldn't think of him as savagely beautiful.

Alex snorted. "You can pull anything off, huh?"

Constantine stepped aside for us to come in, and I noticed no pants legs were visible beneath his robe, and I knew he always went commando.

I didn't wear panties or a bra for this either, and I was suddenly too aware of my nipples pushing through the cotton of my T-shirt.

Constantine motioned at an armchair and end table at the foot of the bed. They weren't here yesterday. "Thought you'd be more comfortable with some semblance of a distance," he said.

Whether he meant Alex or me, I appreciated his thoughtfulness.

Alex sat, and Constantine produced a bottle of whiskey from his nightstand and filled a glass for him. He cocked an eyebrow at me. *"Liquid courage?"* he asked in my head.

"Yes, please," I replied in the same manner. I downed the drink he poured me and enjoyed the burn, though the buzz from the alcohol fumes would only last a few minutes. Could we make this quick? We had to reach orgasm for the ritual to work, but that didn't take long with Constantine.

Constantine took the empty glass from me, set it aside, and held out his other hand. "Shall we?"

Unsure what else to do, I placed my palm in his.

He twirled me so my back was flush against him, and brought his arms around me, to skate his palms up my thighs. My body's reaction was immediate. I leaned into him, molding to his hard planes. Giving him the lead in our dance.

He rocked his hips, and I let him sway me to his silent rhythm, as he popped the button of my jeans and lowered the zipper. His hard cock dug into the small of my back. I stood on tiptoe, so he'd rub against my ass instead. When he slid his fingers under my T-shirt, I sucked in my stomach, every muscle in my body tense with equal parts anticipation and trepidation. He was the same temperature as me, but his touch set my skin on fire. And Alex could see it.

Constantine chuckled. "Relax."

Right. Alex knew what we were here for.

Constantine nuzzled my cheek and grazed my sides with his fingertips, before closing his large palms over my breasts. His touch was gentle yet confident. He knew my body and remembered what I liked, but he gave me ample opportunity to stop him before he pinched my nipples.

I didn't.

He slipped one hand down my belly and inside the waist of my jeans, to cup my pussy. I pumped my hips forward, willing him lower, but his fingers stilled against my bare flesh.

"This won't be fast," he said, twisting and tugging on one of my nipples until I ached with need. "I have one last time to savor you, and I intend on taking full advantage of it. Unless there are any objections."

I looked at Alex for a reaction; he must have heard Constantine's words.

Alex's expression was unreadable.

Another choice for Cherry to make, then.

I lifted my head and rubbed my cheek against Constantine's. I wanted this as much as he did, and if I was to have something real with Alex, I couldn't hide from him. "No objections"—I was glad I hadn't fed and they couldn't see my embarrassment painted in red all over my face—"but I want you both."

Alex narrowed his eyes and tilted his head. "At the same time?"

"Yes." I didn't expect to have to talk things out.

"Not yet, though." Constantine pushed his hand lower and ran one finger along my slit.

I squeezed my thighs together, trapping him in place until I got a response from Alex.

It took an eternity, but Alex said, "Okay."

Constantine turned me around and tugged off my T-shirt, his fingers lingering on my breasts. I stood before him topless, and he claimed my lips with the same fervor he had on the night he admitted to forging a mental link between us.

And he messed with my head tonight as much as he did then.

If I were to decide now, I'd choose to stay with him. Luckily, my mind was already made up.

He broke the kiss and caught my gaze before helping me lie on the bed. It was custom made so he could fuck standing up—his words—which he demonstrated on several occasions. I had no doubt it was what he had in mind now. I kicked off my flats, closed my eyes, and lifted my hips so he could peel off my jeans. My bravado had been spent on my request and had taken with it all other initiative.

When an eternity passed and Constantine hadn't touched me, I opened my eyes to find him staring down at me. Violet flecks wound around his irises, and his fangs were out.

He was hungry. Starving. For me.

I stopped caring about the ritual, the prophecy, ever becoming human again. My sole purpose was to sate his hunger. I was wet and aching for him. I dipped two fingers between my lower lips and brought them to my mouth, to taste myself.

Constantine growled, and Alex echoed him, as he appeared next to him.

Alex's gaze was dark, but I wasn't afraid. It wasn't jealousy swimming in the depths of his grey eyes, but desire. He pulled his shirt over his head and sent it flying across the room. Hard muscle rippled and flexed, as he undid his jeans and stepped out of them.

I looked at Constantine. "You should be naked too."

He untied the sash and let his robe slide off his shoulders and float to the floor. Next to Alex's tan skin, Constantine looked like he was carved from living marble.

They were night and day and all mine.

Whether Constantine's idea worked as planned or not, this would be the best night of my existence.

Constantine lifted one of my legs and laid an open-mouthed kiss over the ankle. He glided his mouth up my calf and kissed the back of my knee, as he pushed me higher up, so he could climb on the mattress between my legs.

I raised my head, wanting to see him, but Alex hopped on the bed next to me and leaned down for a kiss that left my lips swollen.

Constantine trailed more kisses up my thigh, ignoring my barked orders to go higher still. He took his time nibbling on the tender flesh, and then moved his attentions to my other leg, never touching my aching center.

I reached for his hair, intending to use it as a lever, but Alex grabbed both my wrists and pinned them to the mattress, over my head. His cock nudged my hip, teasing me.

Constantine recaptured my attention by spreading my legs as wide as they'd go and laying a kiss on my pussy.

"Finally," I said.

Constantine shook his head. "Oh, I'm going to make you beg for it."

It didn't take long.

He alternated between flicking my clit with his tongue and sucking on it. He grazed it with his teeth. Pushed his tongue inside me. The sensations drove me to the edge but weren't enough to send me tumbling over it.

Alex kept me in place, his hands on my wrists and a leg pressing down on my knee. I was exposed and needy, and I couldn't get enough of their divine torture.

Which I'd never experience again.

The thought was sobering, but I forgot about it when Constantine worried my clit with his teeth and tapped it with the tip of his tongue.

"Please," I sent through our link. Out loud I added, "More."

Constantine laughed and sat back on his haunches. I thought he wanted me to beg aloud, and I was about to do just that, when he thrust two long, thick fingers in my pussy. I pumped my hips, and he leaned over me to close his lips over my nipple. He hooked his fingers inside me and began slamming his palm against me, so the heel rubbed against my clit.

His fangs descended again, piercing the skin around my nipple, and making me arch into his mouth.

Alex let go of one wrist and pinched my second nipple punishingly. I stretched and grabbed his hard cock. It throbbed in my fist. I couldn't focus on him, though, because my mind—my entire being—was rolled in a ball in my cunt, waiting to erupt through my cells.

I was close. So close.

Constantine fucked me with his hand, rubbing against the bundle of nerves inside while pressing on my sensitive button. I pulsed in time to his thrusts, tasting release but not attaining it.

I let Alex's cock slip out of my grasp. I didn't trust myself not to dig my nails into him. He nuzzled my neck and kneaded my breast, but that wasn't what I yearned for.

In my head, I chanted, *"Please. Please. Please..."*

A million times, I must have said it, before Constantine thought at me, *"Since you ask so nicely..."* He pressed the heel of his hand down on my clit and mentally said, *"This is how I want to remember you. Falling apart with pleasure. For me."*

My body shook with the force of the orgasm that tore through me. I had to clench my jaw, to keep from screaming as white-hot fire radiated from my core to every one of my nerve endings.

I lost control over my senses, and the sounds of the night above reached my ears despite the relative soundproofing of the room. An owl. A passing car. Wesley's heartbeat two floors above us. I was grateful not to catch the scent of the women who lived here till recently. I only smelled Alex and Constantine. Their arousal. Precum dripping from their cocks. My blood.

Constantine slanted his lips over mine, and I tasted myself on his tongue, before melting into his kiss. I dug my hand in his bun and loosened it, letting his golden mane cascade down his shoulders.

"That was amazing," he said out loud.

I didn't answer, too busy regaining my bearings.

And then he flipped me on my stomach.

Stars blinked behind my eyelids when I slid them shut.

Constantine licked down my spine, and his tongue sent tingles along my fingers and toes. His hair tickled my skin. He gave my ass a playful bite, and I shook it with a giggle.

Alex got out of bed and stood in front of me. He fisted his hand in my hair, and tugged me upward. When I propped myself up on my elbows, he found his way into my mouth. This time I paid his cock better attention. I swirled my tongue over the tip, and sucked until my cheeks hollowed. He moaned and pumped his hips against my face, and I touched my teeth to the underside, the way I knew he liked it.

Constantine straddled my legs, and his erection poked at me. Why was he wasting time? Why wasn't he already inside me?

I tried to lift my hips, but he slapped my ass.

Nice.

One slicked finger—saliva?—separated my buttcheeks and pressed against my asshole. I bucked. I'd said I wanted him and Alex at the same time, but I didn't like things going up my ass. Well, except a couple times, when Alex's fingers were more adventurous than usual.

But I couldn't take Constantine's cock.

I mean, have you seen that thing? It was too big for back there, but it perfectly matched my pussy, that craved him desperately.

"You said you wanted both of us," he whispered in my mind. *"I chose first."*

Alex didn't pause his thrusts, and I couldn't speak around the dick in my mouth, so I sent Constantine, *"Don't hurt me."*

"Do you want me to stop?" he sent back.

Maybe? *"Why choose to go there?"* I asked.

"I saw your face contort in bliss for me. I want to hold on to that memory, not watch while life seeps out of you."

Sold. *"Do it."*

He pushed his finger in, past the tight ring of muscle, and I bit my lip. I'd gone this far with Alex and enjoyed it. I forced myself to push back into it until I felt Constantine's knuckles against my pussy. He withdrew slowly, and my flesh gave way more easily when he inched back inside. Soon he was sliding his finger in and out of my ass at the same time Alex fucked my mouth.

Constantine tried to add a second finger, but my body clenched around him. He tilted up my hips and buried himself inside my pussy in one hard thrust. My inner walls fluttered at the intrusion, and he took advantage of my surprise, to drive his second finger in my ass. And it was good. Scratch that—it was great. His cock hit all the right spots, and his fingers in my ass added to the delicious feeling of being filled.

Alex closed his fist over his cock and slipped it out of my mouth. I flattened my upper body to the mattress, watching as he moved his hand lazily along his shaft, like he didn't want to come yet. Of course. He'd soon be inside me too.

Yes.

I met Constantine's thrusts, feeling each down-stroke like a jolt of electricity to my core. I was seconds from coming again.

And then the bastard pulled out.

My mewl of frustration turned into a groan when he positioned the tip of his cock at my asshole. He squeezed the first inch inside, and I wasn't all that thrilled. It burned and stretched me, and I didn't see what people liked about it.

He stilled. "Tell me when you want me to move."

Never?

I nodded and twisted my hands in the sheets. I once wanted to be a porn star, damn it; I could handle anal. And I trusted Constantine to make it good. "I'm okay," I said.

He drove forward slowly, stopping every so often to caress my back or use our link to tell me I'm beautiful and that the memory of this moment would get him hard for years to come. He didn't let his sexy talk get sentimental, but his touch reminded me of how he felt. How he said he'd always feel.

It was too much. *"Can you be quiet?"* I thought at him. *"I'm trying to focus on taking your huge dick in."*

He chuckled and brushed my hair out of the way to kiss the back of my neck, then sent me a mental image of himself buried in my ass. *"Beautiful."*

It kind of was.

He withdrew as slowly as he entered me, until only the tip was inside, and then sheathed himself inside me again, with a little more force. He kept going until the near-unbearable discomfort deepened into a different kind of ache. The burning sweetened into pleasure. The stretching made me feel full and yet want more. *This* was what people loved about it.

A few more lunges, and I was impaling myself on him with abandon. *"So good."* I fed on people and played with their memories, but *this* felt like the naughtiest, dirtiest thing I'd done. And I couldn't get enough. I was a fucking convert.

Constantine laughed and snaked his hand around my hip. I thought he meant to find my clit and send me headfirst into another spiraling release, but he grasped me and used his vampire strength to flip us over.

Ah.

I draped my legs back over Constantine's and arched an eyebrow at Alex.

He didn't need more of an invitation. He crawled between our spread legs and ran his hand up the length of my body. He palmed my breast, and I held his gaze as I closed my fingers around his shaft and guided him inside my pussy. He entered me in one smooth stroke. When I felt his balls slam against Constantine's, I expected one of them to recoil, but neither seemed perturbed or inclined to stop.

My body fought to contain the men stretching and filling me. I thrashed between them, while they found their rhythm, seeking their pleasure in my body. Their cocks rubbed against each other through the thin barrier of my flesh. The sensation hurtled me toward new heights of desire. I wanted them to fuck me raw. To rip me apart and put me back together.

One pushed forward while the other withdrew, never leaving me empty. They moved and positioned me, to better accommodate them. They pinched and caressed every inch of skin they could reach. Fingers dug in my hips. Spread my pussy. Scratched my thighs. Alex lifted my leg, so he could go deeper. Constantine knotted his fist in my hair and pulled to the side, exposing my neck. Mouths closed over my flesh—one nibbling, one piercing. I was a piece of clay, there for them to shape at will. And I loved it.

The stinging in the crook of my neck, where Constantine was feeding on me, pulsed in time to the tugging in my womb. My fangs itched. I locked my gaze with Alex's, and he knew what I wanted.

He leaned down and threw back his head, and I sliced into his shoulder, careful to stay away from major blood vessels. His blood filled my mouth, but I let it dribble down my chin, instead of swallowing. I needed to die on Constantine's lips, shuddering in pleasure around him, before Alex's blood brought me back.

But I wanted to feel this connection to Alex now.

I was seconds from coming again, and could tell neither of the men was far behind. Their thrusts turned shorter. Jerkier. No longer timed to flow together. They pounded me into each other, chasing their completion, and I was in heaven in our jumble of need.

Panic threatened to overtake me when I realized I was no longer moving, just lay there, impaled between the men I loved, as they gave me pleasure and took away my life.

I swallowed down the fear and trusted them to bring me back from this. I wanted to tell Alex it was okay. That we'd make it. My fangs retracted, but my lips were too numb to form words.

Blood loss, pleasure, and Alex's weight on me made my body heavy and my head light. My mind spun, as Constantine—or maybe Alex—found my clit and rubbed.

"I love you," Constantine said in my head. And then, "Now, Alex."

The last things I felt as I shattered in a million pieces were cool cum spilling inside me and a coppery taste on my lips.

Then I fell… fell… fell... into darkness.

Chapter Ten

Who the fuck was hammering?

No. Not hammering.

Blunter. Softer.

A thudding. What was it?

I opened heavy eyelids, to look around. The sound came from close by.

Me.

My heart.

My heart was beating.

I heaved in a breath and felt my lungs expand. I'd forgotten the need to do this. I held my breath for as long as I could, but my lungs constricted, sending the air whooshing out my nose. My *human* lungs. My *human* nose.

I was fucking human again.

And I was back in my jeans and top. My feet were tangled in satin sheets. I was still in Constantine's bed. I stretched, my soles gliding against the smoothness, and bumped my ass against something that yielded. Someone.

"I think she's awake."

I rolled around and saw Alex sitting on the bed next to me, fully dressed. If it weren't for the throbbing in my pussy, I might worry the naughty fun-times he and I shared with Constantine—that Constantine and I shared with Alex— were a dream.

"Hey," I whispered. My throat was raw. I touched my neck gingerly. *Ouch.* There was no stickiness or gaping wounds where Constantine bit me, but the muscle beneath the skin felt battered.

"Hey." Alex smiled and brought my hand to his lips, to lay a gentle kiss on my knuckles. "How are you feeling?"

"Alive." I returned the smile and sat up. Ouch. My ass was sore too. Still, I loved the reminders of last night. Having Alex and Constantine inside me at the same time was incredible.

More—it worked.

And how did I feel about that?

Alex was as excited as a puppy in a ball pit. "We're human again, Cherry. Or do I call you *Gerri* now on? I can get used to *Gertrude*, if I have to, but I prefer Gerri. It's more you." He pulled me in his arms. "We can have a life together. I know we talked about it, but it's really real. I can hear your heart beat. You're *warm*, baby."

"I know." I hugged him more tightly but let my smile slip. My chest felt hollow. Empty. Which was weird, since I felt my heart batting against my ribs.

Constantine sat in the armchair, staring at me as if searching for something. It might be the same thing I was missing.

"Can you still hear me?" I asked in my head.

The void inside widened at his silence.

"Constantine?"

Nothing.

"When do you want to move?" Alex whispered in my ear.

Constantine's eyes burned holes in my soul, the sadness in them near-palpable.

"Today," I whispered back.

Constantine gave a tiny nod, and I returned it. I would respect his wishes.

He stood and mouthed *goodbye*. My stomach churned. I didn't miss this from my human days. I hid my face in Alex's neck and squeezed my eyes shut. My connection to Constantine was severed.

I heard the door of his room open and close. He couldn't hear me, but I sent, *"I'm sorry."*

* * * *

Packing to leave Constantine's mansion was hard. Knowing I could never return had me close to tears the entire time Alex and I folded clothes and shoved them in our bags. Last time I left Constantine, things were different. He'd betrayed me. This was the other way around, and I didn't feel empowered or validated for breaking his heart like he broke mine.

As if the emotional turmoil wasn't enough, I was friggin' tired by the time we were ready to go. My arms ached, and my back was stiff. Perks of being a mortal. I couldn't begrudge Constantine for not offering to help, and I wouldn't ask Wesley to do manual labor, but I wished we had some supernatural assistance. I should have called the vampettes.

I helped Alex shoulder a third duffle bag, and my stomach made a loud gurgling sound. I let out an embarrassed chuckle. "I think I'm hungry."

Alex snorted. "That thing sounds dangerous."

His snort turned into a chortle, and then a full-out belly laugh. The sound was smooth and round and filled the room. I started snickering and couldn't stop. All the pressure and stress and fear and worry bottled up inside found their way out, until tears squeezed out the corners of my eyes and I was short of breath.

"We need to buy food on the way home," Alex said when we composed ourselves again. "Anything left in my fridge is months past its expiration date."

"I vote we throw away the fridge and get a new one." The memory of Constantine flinging the table into his fridge re-soured my mood, but I shook it off. "I can afford it, with my monthly council salary."

Yeah, baby. I was human and rich.

Feeling awesome about it would kick in any minute now.

Alex arched both eyebrows. "You're gonna keep that?"

"Why not? As far as they know, I'm still a member. If I stay away from them, I'm good." I shrugged. Constantine said he'd cover for me, and I trusted him.

"Cool." Alex grinned. "Ready?"

I picked up my suitcase and held out my free hand. He took it with the one not holding a carryon.

We must have looked funny, burdened down by luggage, but we wanted to make as few trips as possible. Or I did. The sooner I was away from here, the sooner I could start getting over my life as a vampire.

"We should say *goodbye*." Alex tilted his head toward the end of the corridor and Constantine's room.

"Should thank him, too." For putting us up. For helping us turn back to human. For giving me a revelation of a sexual experience.

I let go of Alex, so he could knock on Constantine's door. There was no reply. I turned the handle and pushed, and it slid open, to reveal the empty bed. The armchair and table were gone again.

"Maybe he's upstairs." But I didn't believe it. He'd let me go.

Wesley waited for us at the living room, two small envelopes in hand. One had my name scrawled on it, in Constantine's elegant handwriting, the other Alex's.

"Master Constantine asked me to give you these," the human—hey, that could refer to any of us now; I mean

Wesley—said as he handed them to us. "He requested that you not share their contents."

Sneaky. I was only back with Alex a few hours, and Constantine was making us keep secrets from each other.

Thinking of him as sneaky made it easier to act disinterested as I flipped open the envelope and pulled out a folded piece of paper.

Forgive me for not being strong enough to walk you out of my eternity. I love you. ~C

I sniffed, folded the note again, and slid it back in the envelope. As I pushed it in my back pocket, I caught Wesley's gaze. His face was pinched, his eyes red. He was an old man when I met him, but now he seemed ancient. Gaunt. Crumbling.

Without thinking about it, I dropped the suitcase and squeezed him in a tight hug. He felt frail.

After a heartbeat, he squeezed back. "Don't let him convince you he's fine," he whispered in my ear. "He's not. He needs you, and soon he'll need you more."

There was nothing to say to that. I blinked tears away and gave him a peck on the cheek. "I'll miss you."

He trained his gaze to the ground. "I'm sorry to see you go, but I wish you both the best."

We thanked him, and Alex got the door for me. My first step outside was underwhelming. The sun was warm against my skin, but it'd been that way since shortly after I started taking Ruby's potion. The colors hadn't changed either. Good that my first experience with the outside as a human wasn't at night. I'd miss the colors only vampires saw, even if I told Constantine otherwise.

I drew a long breath. Now *this* was different. The air didn't taste of pollution as much. It felt fresh. Rejuvenating. I slipped my hand into Alex's.

He turned a huge grin my way. "Let's get something to eat, and then make plans."

I grinned back. "Sounds good."

We got in his Chrysler and buckled our safety belts. How funny would it be if we managed to become mortal again, only to die in a car crash the same day?

Not funny at all. What's the matter with you?

His note from Constantine peeked out of his shirt pocket.

I pointed at it. "Yours any good?"

Alex slid me a sideways glance.

"Okay. No talking about the notes. Whatever." My stomach made another of those freaky sounds, and my mouth felt full of cotton. "Huh. I'm thirsty too." Human thirst was different to bloodlust. It wasn't all consuming. Just a nagging reminder that I had to have some liquid. I ran the tip of my tongue over my canines. If I were still a vampire, these would be way longer by now—I was hungry, thirsty, and in close proximity to a hot human male.

I wasn't a vampire any more, and I should stop comparing my old reality to this one.

"Burger and a milkshake?" Alex asked as he passed the open gates.

I tried hard not to look behind. "I don't feel like it. How about pizza?" I doubted I'd ever want a burger again. I'd forever associate them with Constantine.

"Sounds good."

And then we'd talk plans. I hoped he wouldn't mention getting engaged again for a very long time. I loved him, but we weren't *there* yet.

I flipped down the sun visor and slid aside the cover of the mirror, to keep myself busy.

And then I shrieked.

Alex hit the brakes. "What? What?"

Honking filled the air, and I said, "Don't stop. It's just—" The woman looking at me from the mirror had thin lines around her eyes and several inches of graying blonde roots. *Which made no sense*, because my hair wasn't any longer than it had been since Willoughby turned me.

And yay to that, by the way. If my hair showed six years' worth of growth, so would my nails, and there'd be a lot of waxing in my immediate future. *Ew, ouch*, and *eek* at the same time.

He glanced at me as the car started moving again. "You're beautiful."

"I'm *thirty*."

He laughed. "There's worse. And you're a hot thirty."

I examined my reflection. It wasn't *that* bad; if it happened gradually, I probably wouldn't notice. But it was all at once. Should we skip pizza and go to a beauty salon?

My stomach said *no*.

I expected Alex to stop at a chain pizza place, but he pulled over at the first Italian restaurant we came across.

"Not sure we'll find milkshakes here," I murmured, trying to figure out if my hair looked better in a ponytail. Closer study indicated the color was faded, not grown out. And was it me, or was it no longer perfectly straight?

Alex reached in the map pocket on the driver's side and pulled out a deep blue jockey hat. He held it out to me. "Now can we eat?"

"Yup." I put it on and arranged my bangs under the visor. Not bad, as long as the Italian place wasn't too classy.

My mom told me once that ladies weren't supposed to remove their hats while eating. I'm pretty sure she didn't mean jockeys and was talking about the distant past, but it'd do.

The restaurant was small and cozy, and nobody looked at us twice, even when we ordered two family pizzas. I devoured the first slice before I paid attention to the taste. When I did, I was bummed out. I always loved pepper and added extra to most dishes, but this wasn't a case of the pizza needing a boost of spice. It was loaded with peperoni and sprinkled with jalapenos, and yet it lacked oomph.

"Is something wrong?" Alex asked.

"The flavors are understated. Blunter than I'm used to."

He gobbled down a huge bite. "Tastes fine to me."

Because he'd only been a vampire a short while. Not long enough for his flavor buds to adjust permanently. I could pretend it was my pizza's fault and other things would taste normal, but I knew better.

Still—human, back with a guy I loved, and about to splurge on myself and on renovating his apartment for us. It was all good.

"Let's go shopping," I said, feigning enthusiasm for my food.

"For…?"

"Everything. Clothes, shoes, furniture… But first I have to fix this mess." I indicated my head with a twirl of my finger.

"Your face?"

I glared, before I saw the glint in his eyes. "*My hair*," I said pointedly, but couldn't keep the corners of my lips from tugging up.

Alex reached across the table and took my hand in both of his. "Are you okay with this?"

"With the pizza, or with you implying I need plastic surgery?" By the way, I could finally get some work done. *Hello lipo and new boobs.*

"You know what I mean." When he was in detective mode, there was no changing the subject.

I shrugged and guzzled my soda. "It'll take some getting used to, but I'm more than okay." Except there was a pressure low on my belly I hadn't felt in a while. I jumped up, jostling the table. "Be right back," I said, and ran to the ladies' room.

Running full speed was weird too, like I waded through Jell-O. But the weirdest thing ever was peeing for the first time in half a dozen years. I thought it'd never end. And I'll spare you the horror that's the Ladies' Room Experie—

No, wait. I won't. It's *horrible*. You can't touch anything. Can't sit down. If you're an idiot like me and keep your cell phone in your back pocket, you have to tuck it under your chin and pray it stays put. *While you're hovering over the toilet with your knees half bent.* Killer exercise for the thighs and glutes.

At least the place seemed clean, smelled fresh, and had toilet paper.

I washed my hands and returned to the table.

Alex managed three quarters of a pizza, but I stopped halfway through the third slice.

He sat back and rubbed his stomach. "I'd missed feeling full after a shitload of carbs," he said.

"I know, right?" I popped the button on my jeans. That was something I could do without. I'd have to start watching my diet. My only consolation was that it'd be easier with food tasting like cardboard.

"So what'll you do with your hair?"

Alex's question threw me. "Retouch the red? Maybe grow out the bangs."

"Why don't you go blonde again? It suited you." He'd seen an old picture in my missing person's file shortly after we met.

"It washed me out," I said.

"It'll be different. A fresh start."

A human start. A worrisome thought dawned on me. "Are you trying to erase the woman who… who was in that room, with you and Constantine?"

"No." He answered immediately, but it was the shock in his eyes that convinced me he was being honest. "God, no. If it weren't for *that* woman, I wouldn't have *this* woman with me."

"You know it's the same woman, right? I'm me?"

"I know. And every moment of your life has shaped you. That includes last night, which was mind blowing."

"So it didn't bother you to watch me with Constantine?" I whispered.

He grimaced. "It wasn't my favorite thing ever, but it was necessary."

Time for brutal honesty. "It wasn't necessary for me to be so into it."

He squeezed my leg under the table. "You never denied having feelings for Constantine, and the man makes me bi-curious. Plus, I'd be an ass if I wanted you to have sex you didn't like. What matters is that you're here now. You chose to be with me."

About that… "I decided to go through with the change before you and I said we'd get back together."

"Same result." He leaned closer and brushed his thumb over my cheekbone.

This Alex 2.0 was a curious beast, but I liked how he made me feel about myself and our relationship.

"I'll go blonde," I said.

Chapter Eleven

My stomach churned again, and it had nothing to do with the lustful gazes the colorist doing my high- and low-lights threw Alex.

He looked at odds with the pink hues of the salon's waiting room, but I bet what caught Mircella's gaze wasn't his drab attire, but his gorgeous grey eyes, wide mouth, and sculpted upper body. If he were standing, my bets would be on his ass. Bitable. Seriously.

What would Mircella think, if I told her I spent last night with him and a possibly even hotter male specimen?

No thinking of that. Constantine wanted out of my life; he'd stay out of my head too. Technically, he already was.

I covered my mouth and swallowed a very unladylike burp. Whatever magic kept vampire bodies going after death, conveniently disappeared all sorts of waste in the process.

Being a human was messy. My armpits were sweaty—because who would remember to use body spray after not needing it for this long?—and I still tasted the pepperoni. It might be good my taste buds weren't sensitive now, or I wouldn't make through the day without hurling.

Ugh.

I was in serious need of antacids.

Alex caught my gaze in the mirror and smiled.

I returned it. He was so nice to wait for me, instead of spending his time at the electronics' store.

Of course, I waited for him first.

And I shouldn't go there.

A stylist approached us and introduced herself as Gretchen. "Do you have something specific in mind?" she asked.

"I was thinking of growing out my fangs—*bangs*, so maybe layer it a bit? I don't know. Whatever you think will suit me."

Her eyes glazed over with creative mania. "How about an asymmetrical long bob with sidebangs?"

Why not? It was just a hairstyle. Temporary. "Do it."

By the time I was done, I was a new me. Not the girl who left San Luis Obispo to make a career in showbiz, and not the vampire who fucked two men last night.

Loose curls framed my face, one side down to my chin, the other reaching my collarbone. Gretchen did a good job of thinning my bangs and swiping them to the side, so they were half hidden. The overall color was a honey blonde, with pale-beige and light-chestnut streaks. And I loved it.

I thanked the ladies who performed this miracle, paid, and strutted over to Alex.

"Ya like?" I turned this way and that, for him to take in the amazeballs that was my new look.

He stood and pulled me flush against him. "You're gorgeous."

Mircella must have noticed the ass on the man, because she gave me a thumbs-up as I slid my hand in his back pocket.

I felt good, as we strolled out of there. Kind of proud of myself too, for only wondering once what Constantine would think of my makeover. He always liked redheads.

"Next up, nails." If I never painted them red again, it'd be too soon.

Alex shook his head. "I've been around enough estrogen for a day. I'll drive you where you need me to, and then make a couple calls. Maybe swing by my place and empty the fridge. You call me when you're done, and I'll pick you up."

"Okay." A quick search returned the info of three nail salons in the area, and the third one had an opening for an emergency mani-pedi.

Add waxing, and my second first day as a human would be pretty much the same as my first last one.

Lost you, huh?

After my nails, I caught a taxi to the mall. I got *some* groceries, also known as crackers and cheese, and then did some damage with my recently acquired credit card. If the thing had a limit, I didn't find it.

Alex pulled up at the mall's northern entrance, got out, and popped the trunk for me to stash my shopping.

I noticed our luggage wasn't in the back seat. "You unloaded the car?"

"And put everything away. Had enough time to kill." He hummed with pent up energy and seemed more upbeat than when I left him, as he got the passenger door.

"Everything okay?" I asked, as I sank into my seat and carefully laid my brand-sparkling-new Balenciaga bag on my lap—thank you, vampire council.

"More than okay. Perfect. Incredible." He took me in and wolf-whistled. "And I get to take you home."

It was hard to resist his good mood, and I had no reason to try. Things were pretty great. Years ago, I left my home town to make something of myself. Today, I could get started on that, and I didn't have to worry about money. And this hunk of a man was taking me home.

He slammed my door shut and rounded the car to get behind the wheel. I closed my hand over his on the gear stick as he went into first gear. I loved that he drove stick. Gave me an illusion of control over the mechanic beast we rode in. I buckled up again, and we headed for his apartment.

Home.

And I'd never even seen the place.

"So your mysterious calls panned out?" I asked. "Or is this the face of a man with a clean fridge?"

He chuckled. "Both. The fridge wasn't an issue after all."

"And the calls?"

"Don't you want to wait till we're home and can properly celebrate?"

"Tell me. Now. Now now now."

He caressed my little finger with his thumb and shifted to second gear. "I have my job back. Roebuck wants me in, first thing Friday morning."

Day after tomorrow. "He couldn't give us the weekend?" I pouted, but stopped when I remembered I was a thirty-year-old woman now.

Alex let go of the gear shift to give my thigh a gentle squeeze. "He doesn't know this is our first week with a heartbeat. Last we spoke, I demanded he suspend me."

It was Alex's way of keeping his people out of harm's way while he and I looked for Willoughby. After my neighbor Dotty, whom Willoughby kidnaped to shut me up, resurfaced and couldn't give the cops anything about her mystery kidnapper, Alex asked for more time off, to get over his supposed failure.

"He has no hard feelings?" I asked.

Alex gave a small shrug. "He sounded happy to hear from me, and I can usually read him. He said it was about time I pulled my head out of my ass and got with the program."

"Wise man."

Alex snapped his jaws at me, and I laughed. Then something worrisome crossed my mind. "He didn't demote you." Being a detective wasn't safe, but I'd take that over the hazards wearing a uniform entailed.

"Nah. Nothing's changed. It's like the past few months never happened."

But they did.

I tried to keep my mouth shut and failed. "Try not to take any unnecessary risks?"

"You know they're part of the job." We stopped at a traffic light, and he turned to study my face. "Can you handle it?"

I'd known from the beginning that his life was on the line much of the time, but back then he didn't mean this much to me. And then he died.

The air was jammed in my lungs at the memory of watching him bleed to death. The devastation of being unable to save him. The gutting sense of loss, until Constantine brought him back to me...

Alex's death wasn't what I should be thinking of, today of all days. Neither was Constantine. I dug deep for the mood boost that came with the makeover and new clothes—and shoes and cosmetics and a designer bag. "Let's say, if I dump your cute ass, it won't be 'cause of that," I said and immediately regretted it. His ex-fiancée had left him because she couldn't handle his job.

Alex seemed unfazed by my foot-in-mouth moment. Must be getting used to me. "Good to know, but there's not much to worry about. There's a series of muggings gone violent down town he wants me to look into."

That didn't sound too scary.

Alex swerved right, and soon we were leaving traffic behind. Odd. His apartment was in the city, and L.A.'s all about traffic. Odder still, we were heading for the suburbs, down a vaguely familiar road.

When he slowed down, I recognized the street. His mother's house stood near the end of the block. "This is your mom's place," I said.

"Not anymore." He flashed me a grin. "She moved in with Mr. O'Connor while I was in Europe."

"So you get the house?" So many memories in that place. My first night with Alex. Fighting my maker. Falling for Alex.

Losing him.

"*We* get the house. I wanted to surprise you. Is that okay?"

I hadn't lost him. He was right here, beside me.

"*Hell yeah*, that's okay," I said. "There are a couple rooms we haven't fucked in."

Alex left the car with its tail half-hanging out of the driveway, and dragged me to the front door. He fished the key out of his pocket and wedged it in the lock, then shoved the door open until it slammed on the wall behind it.

I let my Balenciaga drop to the floor when he gathered me to him with an arm around my waist. I pulled him down by his lapel, to seal his mouth with mine. While I sucked on his tongue and nibbled on his bottom lip, he undid my jeans and walked me backward to the nearest wall. He inched one hand down the seat of my pants, to cup my ass, and glided the other inside my shirt.

I unbuckled his belt, and was fumbling with his fly when he withdrew both hands with a curse.

"What?" I asked, before noticing the open door. "Oh. Well, close it and get back here."

Alex shook his head while redoing his belt. "Not that. Condoms."

Like a bucket of ice. "Shit. Don't you have any?"

He shook his head again. "I'll be right back."

I kicked the door shut and climbed the stairs to the bathroom. The shower wasn't as quick as I planned. Human-me liked water a lot warmer than vampire-me used to, and I had to keep my hair from getting wet, 'cause it no longer styled itself.

I made it back to the couch and sprawled on it— clean, naked, and grateful for the roll-on deodorant I found in the bathroom cabinet—as Alex reentered the house.

We'd already done it in this room, but oh well.

I motioned him over with my index finger, and he gave me a slow, lazy smile. "I wonder what that means."

I spread my legs. "Come hither."

"Well okay, then." He ripped through the paper bag and box of condoms, and then tore open the condom wrapper with his teeth while he popped his fly one handed. "Let's do this thing."

I laughed. It was good to see him this carefree and silly. And when he pulled his shirt over his head, kicked off his shoes, and dropped his jeans, it was plain good to see him. His midnight-black hair was messy, his grey eyes hooded with desire. His broad shoulders, wide chest, and chiseled abs belonged to a Greek god. I wanted to lose myself in his muscular arms. Feel his wide palms and long fingers map my body. And the rest of him… His legs were long and thick and hard, as was what bobbed between them with every step he took toward me.

He fisted his cock. Two tugs, and he was hard enough to roll the condom down his shaft.

When he knelt with his head between my thighs, I dug my new golden acrylics in his hair and pulled him up my body. "I'm ready for my main course." I needed to connect with him in these new, frail bodies we occupied, as much as I needed to exorcise the ghost hovering at the edge of my consciousness.

Not a ghost. A vampire. Tall and blond and sexy as hell, whose touch lit my body on fire.

I welcomed Alex inside me, pressed my face to his chest and squeezed my eyes against Constantine's memory.

Alex slammed his hips against me. I was still tender from last night, and the pain helped anchor me to the now. My new nails dug furrows that wouldn't heal soon in Alex's back. Skipping foreplay might not be the best idea when I lacked vampire healing, but as we rocked together, the ache faded and soon gave its place to pleasure.

Sex with him remained pretty fucking great. It lacked the intimacy of biting, and it was sweaty and sticky, but he had the moves and knew the right places to pinch and rub and stroke, for me to burst like a rocket. The part where my heart tried to leap out of my chest when I came scared the shit out of me, but hyperventilating added to the euphoria of being properly debauched by Alex.

I only fantasized of Constantine being with us for the briefest of moments.

Chapter Twelve

Alex was ecstatic with my new look, and he was pretty vocal about it, which kept my good mood going after clothes were back on and talk shifted from *I love fucking you* to *so what do we do with our future?*

"You're going back to work on Friday. I should find a job too." I played with the thin line of hairs beneath his navel. I lay on the couch, half on top of him, sweat slicking our skin and melding us together.

"I thought you were Ms. Money now. Don't you have a huge allowance for extravagant leather goods?"

I nodded against his chest. "It covers shoes too. But I don't know if anyone keeps track of what comes out of the account. If I use the card for grocery shopping on a regular basis, it may raise flags." Plus, I liked the idea of working again. Weird, I know. Before Constantine dropped the you-can-be-human-again bomb, I didn't mind the rest of my life being a vacation.

"So what will it be?" Alex asked. "Back to modeling?"

"Thought I'd give it a try."

"And the adult movies?"

I sensed the tension beneath his light tone and said, "Nah. I'm over that."

To his credit, he didn't say *good* or anything judgy. "Will you sign with Sheena again?"

I considered it. "She said she'd help me find a job but didn't offer to take me on, and I don't want her to feel like she has to. I'll look for a new agent."

He pulled me closer and kissed the tip of my nose. "Nobody too hot, though." But he was smiling. This wasn't the uncontrollable, irrational jealousy that tore us apart and nearly killed me.

"Define *too hot*." I flicked my tongue over his lower lip. "Someone like you?"

He tangled his fingers in my hair and kissed me hard, but when I closed my fist around his cock, he gently moved my hand away. "Need some time before Round Two."

"Worth the wait." I pressed my lips to his neck, feeling his pulse vibrate beneath the skin.

I don't know which of us drifted off first, but I woke up with a crick in my neck, a stiff lower back, and the pressing need to pee. I climbed over Alex and padded across the carpeted floor and up the stairs to the bathroom. The cold tiles were a shock to my system, but not as bad as the cold water I used, to freshen up once business was done.

"I think there's something wrong with the water heater," I called out on my way downstairs.

"I'll look into it," Alex called back. "Are you dressed?"

I laughed. "Why would I be?"

"Don't worry about me. I've seen it all before," said the woman by the front entrance.

Ruby.

She was dressed in black tights and a long black T-shirt, her auburn hair pulled into a tight low bun. I grew up thinking of her as my awesome aunt, but she was my kickass vampire grandma. And she'd better mean she'd seen *my* all, and not Alex's too.

Alex stood next to her, biting back a smile. He had his jeans on and tossed his T-shirt my way. I snatched it out of the air and pulled it on. Covered to mid-thigh, I hopped the rest of the way down and gave my grandma a hug.

When I pulled away, she was smiling, but tears shone in her dark-brown eyes. "I'm so sorry for everything. I'd have killed Ádísa myself if I knew she'd come after you." Her voice held the faintest hint of an Irish brogue. How did I never notice before? Or was I imagining it now that I knew she was Irish?

"It's okay—umm… What do I call you?"

"I've lost the chance to be your grandma, but you can call me that, if you want. Ruby is fine too."

I studied her. No lines around the eyes. No white hairs. "Ruby for now. It'd be weird calling you Gran, when you look younger than me."

She shook her head. "I watched my husband fade away. I had to uproot my daughter and bring her to a different continent, where she too will grow old and eventually pass on. I'm frozen in time. But you're not. You can be anything you want to be. Have it all." She tilted her head toward Alex and winked at me.

I could also wither and die.

I didn't share the bitter thought.

Alex offered Ruby a drink, which she declined, and we stood there exchanging looks for what seemed like an eternity, before she spoke again.

"Constantine called me. He had me expunge your VSS file." Vampire Social Services—VSS for short—kept records that included details of every registered vampire's turning as well as notes on their whereabouts.

"You can do that?" I asked.

Her grin was smug. "*I* can."

"And nobody will realize?" Alex asked.

"Unless someone requests a hearing, the council holds no meetings in its entirety, for safety reasons," Ruby said. "As long as Gerri avoids seeing them up close, she'll be fine."

Other than getting used to my old name again, it sounded too easy. Not like I'd ever run into any of them by accident. Their hunting grounds were too exclusive for little-old human-me.

"Have you kept your ID?" she asked.

"I have, but can I show it around?"

The smug grin made a reappearance. "You no longer come up as a missing person on electronic records. I didn't manage to follow the paper trail, which means nobody can, and the detective in charge of your case no longer remembers anything about you. So unless you run into a former associate or someone who kept a six-year-old milk carton…"

Alex gathered her in a bear hug before I could. "Thank you. Thank you so much."

I felt like he was trespassing on my sentiment. Stupid, I know, but this was about *me*. I was supposed to be thanking Ruby and squeezing the unlife out of her.

So why were my lips numb when I echoed Alex's gratitude?

Ruby stayed a while longer, to talk with Alex about our future plans and then tell me about places in Europe I absolutely had to visit. Her descriptions of places she traveled to and people she met were so vivid and full of life, I wondered if she realized how much she loved being a vampire.

Her eyes glittered, and her hands drew elegant lines in the air as she spoke of London, Paris, Athens, Rome… "But don't stick solely to big cities. There's a town at the foot of the Carpathians that carries the echoes of German and Hungarian conquerors. The food is divine, and it's got a beautiful little bridge—"

Maybe her previous lamenting of the life she lost was for my benefit. To show me I wasn't missing much by being a mortal.

But I was. Even if I lived to my eighties, which was around the age she'd be if she were human, I'd never lead the life she led till now. I was achy 'cause I slept in an uncomfortable position. I'd never swim naked across the Thames—illegal, by the way—or climb Mount Kilimanjaro.

So what? I had my youth, my health, a man I loved and who loved me, and enough money to do anything I wanted.

Ruby promised to let me break the news to my parents. She said she'd call or write, and then she was off to her hotel or her next adventure. I didn't ask which, and she didn't offer any info.

I felt antsy and exposed. Like my skin was too tight. Too hot. I needed to get dressed. "You said you unpacked?" I asked Alex.

He pointed upstairs. "Master bedroom. Your closet is the one on the right, and I've put lingerie and nightwear in the top two drawers of the dresser."

"Efficient."

"Aim to please."

I blew him a kiss. "You're doing a pretty good job so far."

He gave an exaggerated bow. "So you see exactly how good, I'll even bring in your shopping."

"You're only doing that so I model my new clothes for you."

I was still laughing, when pain sliced my gut and made me double over.

Alex rushed to my side. "Are you okay?" When I didn't answer, he knelt in front of me to meet my gaze.

"Feels like something wrapped its talons in my stomach and pulled," I said through gritted teeth. The description was familiar. *Fuck.* "Can you make a quick supermarket trip?"

He looked at me quizzically.

"I think I'm about to get my period."

* * * *

"Where the fuck are you?" Sheena screeched over the line. "I called the mansion."

"You talked to Constantine?" A dull ache that had nothing to do with period pains settled in my stomach when his name spilled from my lips.

Sheena huffed. "He told me you don't live there anymore. He wouldn't elaborate. Did you have a fight, or…?"

Or. Definitely *or.* He ate me out and fucked me with his fingers and then shoved his magnificent cock up my ass. "Is he okay?" I asked.

"So there *was* fighting?"

"Not the F-ing that transpired, no. But he won't talk to me now, so end result is the same." The ache inside deepened. Widened. Screamed with a need I didn't want to define.

"You fucked him?"

I'd like to correct my previous statement; *now* she was screeching.

I filled the yawning void with excuses—it was better not to see Constantine again; he'd only complicate things; Alex and I were building something together; there was no room for third wheels. Besides, Sheena's exuberance was contagious.

I bit my lip and tried to sound nonchalant, when I was dying to share the deets. "Yup," I said. "Totally did."

"And Alex?"

"And Alex."

"No, I mean how did he take it?"

I tugged at a loose curl. "I did all the taking."

"What are yo— Wait. *You fucked Alex and Constantine? At the same time?*"

I laughed. Ibuprofen was a thing of beauty, for subduing the angry T-Rex in my womb. "I did. And you're going supersonic."

She cleared her throat, and when she spoke next, she sounded more normal. "So what now?"

"Oh, I don't know. I sneezed an hour ago, and I swear an ovary fell off."

"What does that have to do with any—" She gasped. "Shit. You sneezed. *You're human again?*"

I put some distance between the phone and my ear, and yelled, "I am. So is Alex. Now can you please tone down the hysterics?"

"But it's a big thing."

"Inside voice. Please."

Sheena snorted. "Not sure you get to be cranky."

"It's been a long day."

"Sure has. What with fucking two gorgeous men at the same time."

"Yeah, well, I'm being punished for that. Got my period." And one of the men was out of my life for good.

"Shit." She laughed. "Welcome back to the world of the living. Mother Nature knows how to throw one hell of a party."

Alex brought me a cup of hot chocolate. I mouthed *thank you*, and he retreated to the kitchen where he'd been since I heavily implied getting me tampons without an applicator indicated he didn't care.

"Not sure I like being the guest of honor," I told Sheena.

"Oh, hush. You're human again. What's a little blood and pain compared to that?"

I blew on my chocolate and touched my lips to the cup. Too hot to drink, and no marshmallows. Didn't I deserve a good, yummy, *marshmallowy* hot chocolate I could drink?

"There's the bitching too," I said. "Alex isn't happy with me being an emotional mess."

"That's a Cherry thing, not a human thing."

"Fuck you." But I was grinning.

"Well, since you're making the rounds…"

I barked out a surprised laugh. "For shame, woman."

"Yeah, yeah. I'm blushing. But before I forget—now that the visual is fresh in your memory, who's got a bigger cock?"

Her question evoked images of Constantine and Alex naked. Constantine was longer, but Alex was thicker. And I took them inside at the same time. Stretched to accommodate them. Let them fuck me to oblivion.

"Not answering that," I said.

Sheena made a sound of disappointment. "Can I at least know if it was good?"

I peeked toward the kitchen, made sure Alex wasn't in sight, and then whispered, "It was fucking amazing. I'll walk bowlegged for days, but it was incredible, Sheena." And I wished I could do it again.

"Was there… double penetration? Did you give one of those boys your tight little apple? I mean your ass."

"I know what you mean, and *ew* to that description. Seriously."

"Yeah, you did." She chuckled.

"Yeah, I did."

We acted like horny teens exchanging sex stories for a little longer—well, I did most of the talking, while she gasped, giggled, and made snide remarks.

"And how are you feeling about all of this?" She sounded far more serious than a second ago. I thought she was talking about being human, but she went on. "Back in a relationship with Alex after… I mean it's soon. Moving in together already, cutting all ties to Constantine…"

"That last part wasn't my choice," I said.

"But you're okay with it?"

"Not like I can change things." I hated the waver in my voice. "He's right, if you think about it. I'll eventually see things his way."

"Are you over him?"

The question landed like a slap on my face. The painkillers were wearing off, my lower abdomen hurt, and my gut churned. I should take something for this. "I thought I was."

"And now?"

Now I had to be.

Alex came in, to ask if I needed anything else. I shook my head and smiled at him, and he laid a kiss on my forehead before getting his car keys. "I'll get some food," he whispered.

I shoved Constantine's memory aside, squeezed it into a tiny little box and buried it where it wouldn't mess with me. "I love Alex," I told Sheena when Alex was out the door. "I'll make it work."

She must have caught on to my need to change the subject, because she said, "Any plans for tomorrow? Wanna get lunch?"

"How about Friday? I want to cook for Alex tomorrow, to make up for all the nagging." And for missing Constantine.

I could practically hear Sheena roll her eyes, as she said, "May the Lord have mercy on that boy."

Chapter Thirteen

I'd woken up next to Alex several times before, but this was entirely new, and not because of the foul taste in my mouth.

Alex was spread out across the bed as usual, one leg across mine, and an arm on my stomach. It was annoying when I was a vampire, but sweltering hot when we were both above room temperature and under the sheets.

I slid out of bed and hurried to the bathroom, to brush my teeth and relieve the pressure in my bladder. I hated the human morning routine. As a vampire, all I did most mornings was sleep through them.

All freshened up, I slipped back into bed. Alex had rolled away. I ran my hand down the length of his body, but he lay still. I listened for his heartbeat, panicked, and then remembered I couldn't hear heartbeats anymore.

I pressed closer until his heart thudded against my chest. Or maybe it was the other way around. I wedged my arm underneath his and wrapped it around his waist.

"Are we being naughty or cuddly?" he asked.

"Cuddly." I rubbed my nose between his shoulder blades. It was too hot under the covers. I flicked them up and folded a leg over them. Better. Now I could stay like this for a couple minutes.

"I love waking up with you again," he said.

I nodded against his skin. A trickle of sweat tickled the small of my back. Couple of minutes had to be up. "I need coffee." I laid a kiss on his shoulder and got out of bed.

"Me too. And something to eat."

"Grilled cheese okay? Lunch will be something more elaborate. Honest."

He laughed and kicked the sheets away. I stole a glimpse of his naked body as he strolled to the bathroom. His morning arousal was unaffected by his breathing status.

I went down the stairs with a smile on my face that wilted when I saw the dirty dishes in the sink. They were a couple of plates and three glasses, but the last few months with Wesley around and a cleaning service on call had spoiled me.

I turned on the coffee maker and got to washing up. I was living here rent free; I could at least help with the chores, though I planned on covering my share of utilities and expenses too. Alex and I had to have a talk.

"Will you take out the trash?" I asked when he came down in a pair of boxer shorts. He smelled amazing, and if it weren't for the current no-entry policy in my lady parts, I'd be all over him.

"Can it wait for after breakfast?"

"Sure." I covered four slices of bread with grated cheddar and put them in the oven, then turned on the grill.

Alex poured us two cups of coffee, added a heap of sugar to mine, and brought our mugs and a carton of milk to the table. I towel dried the dishes while waiting for the cheese to melt.

"I was thinking I should chip in. I mean, if I'm going to live here, I need to pay my way. Cover half of the utilities. Maybe a little extra, since I'm not paying rent?"

Alex looked at me like I'd grown a second head. "You're not paying rent *because you're my girlfriend.* I'm not going to take money from you for staying here. We can share the bills, yeah, but no more than that."

"Okay. Cool. Yeah." It still felt weird. I had no problem not paying for anything while we stayed at the mansion, but Constantine didn't need the money. "And I'll pay for half of the new furniture we get."

"Like half a sofa, half a table, and so on?"

I smacked the back of his head with the dishtowel, then used it to take our breakfast out of the oven.

"This isn't a sandwich," Alex said when I placed his plate in front of him.

"It's an open-faced sandwich."

"So a slice of bread."

"Two slices."

He waggled his eyebrows. "Still not a sandwich."

I grabbed one slice and flipped it over the other. "There. Now it is."

Alex laughed, and I joined him. This was nice. Relaxed. Fun. Couple-y. I'd stick to it, and soon my blood-drinking days would be behind me, and I'd stop comparing *now* to *then*.

We spent the rest of the day watching TV shows—I may have developed an unhealthy attraction to a fictional demon hunter—and talking about mundane things like leasing out his apartment and transferring the house's utilities to his name.

My belly hurt, but the pain was dulled. The same should eventually happen to the sense of loss that came with scratching out the last few years of my existence.

Lunch was late and consisted of a pretty *not* bad Salisbury steak and mashed potatoes that came out of a box. I was proud of myself for producing a dish that was neither undercooked nor burned, even if it tasted like boiled chicken to me.

Alex was pleasantly surprised, which would be insulting if I hadn't warned him that we might have to order in.

The small talk flowed between us while we ate, and then I picked up the table, while he went to get chocolate soufflé.

My heart broke a little with the first spoon full, but I finished my portion and thanked him for getting it. And I felt super-petty for thinking he should have known better than to rub my face into my inability to enjoy my once-favorite dessert.

Alex went to the living room, while I stashed the empty patisserie box in the trash. "You didn't take out the garbage," I called out. Yesterday's leftovers were getting rank in the summer heat.

"I will. Come sit with me. You'll miss me tomorrow, when I'm at work."

"Oh, I don't know… I may go furniture shopping." I joined him on the couch, and he made room for me to stretch out beside him. Hot again. I was getting a ceiling fan for each room.

We put on a movie. Took a nap. Ate more. I felt like a lazy bum with an expanding waist line, but Alex and I deserved some peace and quiet.

"Did you call any agencies?" he asked during the first action sequence.

I paused the movie. "When? We've been together all day. Did you see me calling?"

"You're right. Sorry."

"It's okay." I pressed *Play* again

Alex said, "My laptop is upstairs, if you want to look online for modeling agencies."

"Thanks. I will. When the movie is over." I kept my finger over the *Play/Pause* button, waiting to see if he was done.

He wasn't. "I thought you might want to call while it's early in the day. Looks more professional."

Long story short, we didn't see the movie, and I called four agents, the last of which not only picked up her own phone, but also agreed to meet me tomorrow morning.

"I don't feel like a thriller." Alex scrunched his face when I said maybe now we could see the rest. "Wanna try something else?"

I hate, hate, *hate* not watching something to the end, but this was *our* day, and I'd compromise. "Like what?"

"Cooking show?"

I rubbed my full stomach. "No, thank you. I should be cutting down on food, if I ever want to work again."

He placed his hand over mine. "You could join the gym."

Burn.

I diverted my insecurities from his suggestion, and asked, "Comedy?"

"Can't think of any I want to see. You?"

I shook my head.

We watched a basketball game.

Actually, *he* watched it, while I moved my contacts to the new smartphone I bought during yesterday's shopping spree.

I didn't mind the me-time.

I minded that the trash was still in the kitchen.

Human. In love. Good prospects.

Couldn't have everything, but I had a lot.

I took the garbage bag out myself.

It was late, and the first sprinkle of stars lit up the night sky. I sat on the front porch and looked up at them. The darkness felt unfamiliar. The shadows held no shapes I could decipher. No colors blazed through the black.

I knew I'd miss my night vision, but I didn't believe it'd sting so much.

I lay back and folded my hands on my stomach, seeking out the sounds of the night. An owl made its presence known, somewhere nearby. A neighbor's cat meowed. A car engine roared. It all sounded so very far away. So disassociated from me. As an anomaly of nature, I'd felt more a part of it than I did now that warm blood flowed in my veins.

It'd pass.

I'd adapt. Humans always do; they can't afford not to, with time wearing them down.

The door opened behind me, and seconds later, Alex lay down next to me. "Looking for shooting stars?" he asked.

"Reminiscing," I said.

"Missing the mansion?" Tension lined his voice.

I shrugged and turned to look at him. "If you saw a shooting star now, what would you wish for?"

He propped himself up on his elbow and leaned in, to slant his mouth over mine. "All my wishes have come true," he whispered against my lips.

I kissed him again before he could ask me the same question, because I had no answer for either of us. I loved him, and I loved having a real chance to be with him, but I didn't feel complete, and although I missed Constantine, he wasn't the reason.

I'd made my peace with what Alex had done when he was being used against me, and I felt safe with him again, but the bubble we'd built around us to keep the world out felt restrictive. He was so clear about what he wanted, so determined to move forward, and I still couldn't adjust the shower temperature.

Was something wrong with me? Did my time as a vampire jade me? Was I damaged?

Chapter Fourteen

I was still bloated in the morning. I couldn't zip up my jeans without sucking in my stomach and lying on the bed. It did wonders for my self-esteem, when I was about to visit agencies and ask for work.

An agency. So far, Anastasia Looks was the only one to offer me an appointment. I never heard of them before, but they'd be good for practice. My people skills were rusty from disuse, and I was bloated and pissy. I was cool with starting from the bottom up.

I wore a fitted white T-shirt and checked my hair for the millionth time. Despite my best efforts, my curls came nowhere near what I left the hair salon with, but a few hairpins did wonders for that messy-bun look.

Blazer and pumps on, and I looked good. Polished. Professional.

I was glad Alex left early for work. He didn't need to see more of my insecurities. I texted him, *I'm off.*

My phone chimed a second later. *Good luck. Love you.*

Good thing he did, because Anastasia clearly didn't.

She looked at me over her turtle-shell glasses and tapped a finger on my portfolio, which she hadn't bothered to flip through. "Will your daughter be joining us?"

Huh? "My daughter?"

"Yes. How old is she?"

"I don't have a daughter."

The widening of her eyes was so exaggerated, her surprise was obviously fake. "You mean *you* want to work with us?"

My vampire gaze would come in handy at this point, but I no longer had it, and snark might backfire. I toned down my glare. "I was thinking maybe catalog work. I know runway and editorials have different standards."

"Listen, Ms. Mosby." She said my last name with such disdain, I regretted not using my stage name. "You're what? Thirty-two? Thirty-four?"

"Thirty," I said through gritted teeth.

"Thirty is too old for our industry. Twenty-five is too old. You can't show up now and expect to become a model."

"I've worked as a model before."

"So you say." Her voice dripped disbelief.

I sat straighter. "I have. I did."

She huffed and looked at her smartphone. "Yet you have nothing to show for it. In any case, you're well outside our age bracket."

I pointed at my portfolio. "If you just—"

"Have a nice day." She didn't raise her gaze from her phone.

I was dismissed. Worse, I was humiliated. I snatched my folder and strolled out of there with my head held high, and my stomach sinking lower with each step.

What was a girl to do, to lift her spirits?

Something I wanted for a while.

I scrolled down my contacts list till I reached *P*.

Plastic Surgeon – Dr. King

His receptionist informed me the doctor had no opening for a consultation for another month, but she promised to let me know if there was a cancellation. If she didn't call before Tuesday, I'd drop by and throw cash at her till she fit me in his schedule. Who needed class when I could buy boobs?

The thought of finally getting the upgrades I wanted since I was to star in *Knotting Cherry Stem* made me feel better, but only marginally.

I had the uncontrollable urge to call Constantine and let him know how weird it was to be human after this long. Tell him about the need to pee, and sneezing when there was dust in the room, and fucking menstrual cycles. He might get a kick out of the latter; he was still a bloodsucker.

For four whole years after we broke up, he called me on a daily basis, and for some unexplainable reason I always picked up, if only to tell him to leave me alone. His excuse for ignoring my need for distance was that talking on the phone was different than meeting up close. I could use the same loophole.

I held my thumb over his cell phone number for a second, before I called the mansion instead. The replica of an old rotary phone in the living room had no caller-ID feature. Maybe I'd get lucky and Constantine would pick up.

He didn't. "Good morning. How may I help you?" Wesley's familiar voice sounded tired.

"Hey. It's Cherry. Miss me yet?"

"Of course. The mansion is too quiet without you," he deadpanned.

I laughed. "Does Constantine maybe feel the same way?"

He was silent for a heartbeat or two, and then said, "Master Constantine inquires whether this is an urgent matter."

I could lie and say it was, but it was no use. I kept my voice chipper. "Nah. I wanted to say *hi*. See how he's doing. Maybe tell him about my day."

"I'm afraid he believes keeping in touch is a bad idea. He wishes you the best and asks that you only contact him again in case of emergency."

I swallowed hard and blinked back unbidden tears. "Yeah. I get it."

A door closed somewhere in the background. I was about to say *goodbye*, when Wesley whispered, "Don't give up on him. Please."

I had no warning before a sob burbled up my throat and I could no longer breathe through the snot in my nose. "I got to go," I said.

Wesley wished me a good day and the line went dead.

Constantine was right, I told myself again. I wasn't convinced, but I'd repeat it till I hammered in the need to keep my human life separate from his immortal one. My chest constricted. It felt like my heart stopped beating again. My throat went tight. I gasped for air and leaned against a wall for support until I managed a proper breath.

It would pass. It would all pass, and I'd survive. With Alex by my side. I had him and Sheena, and maybe the vampettes in my corner. And my parents…

I didn't tell my parents I was alive.

I should call now. Or get Alex to drive me over there tomorrow. Or maybe wait until I got the hang of things.

Yeah. No reason to call them yet.

I was staring at my cell phone, when the screen came to life. Sheena. I took the call before the ringtone kicked in. "Hey."

"How did it go?" she asked.

How did she know I called Constantine? *Oh.* She meant the interview that wasn't. I mentioned it in passing last night, when she called to see if Alex survived my cooking. "It didn't go. I'm too old for this shit," I said now.

"I could have told you that."

I frowned. "Great. Kick me when I'm down, why don't you?"

"Cherry, baby, I mean that with love. For all intents and purposes, you're a newcomer to an industry that doesn't take newcomers past their teenage years. You didn't have a strong enough career to call this a comeback, and maybe it's for the best, or people from your past might be suing for breach of contract. Modeling isn't all you can do, though."

I shrugged, though she couldn't see me. I wasn't up for a pep-talk. "Whatever. Are we on for lunch?"

"Sure thing. Meet you there in half an hour."

By *there*, she meant the Italian place Alex and I had our first all-mortal meal at. I'd mentioned it to Sheena, and she wanted to try the pizza. I hoped she'd enjoy it more than I did.

I took a taxi there, got seated, and had a couple glasses of white wine while waiting for her. Not the best idea on an empty stomach, but I didn't mind how it dulled the edges of my thoughts.

Sheena planted a kiss on my cheek and dropped into the chair across from me. I was used to seeing her in bright colors, and this lilac pantsuit seemed too pale against her mocha-color skin. Her black hair was pulled up in a neat bun, with enough product to smooth the kink, and she had on barely-there makeup.

"What's with the transformation?" I asked.

"Trying on a new style. You like?" Before I could answer, she waved the waiter over and pointed at my glass. "We'll have this in bottle form, as well as a large pepperoni pizza."

The man disappeared between tables, while Sheena scrutinized me, her dark eyes narrowed. "What's wrong?"

"Nothing. The job. I didn't like how Anastasia turned me down."

Sheena harrumphed. "You're not seriously letting her get to you."

"It's not just that. It's… I don't know. Everything is so. Fucking. Slow. I can't fly up the stairs, chase someone down, or even get to the kitchen, sneak a snack, and return before Alex knows I'm gone."

Her expression was flat. "I can see how being unable to sneak food past Lover Boy may be upsetting."

"And the shower water's all wrong, no matter how many times I adjust the temperature."

"It would make anyone cranky."

I took a sip of my wine. "You're making fun of me."

"Only 'cause you're being a whiny little shit. You're living my reality. Everyone's reality. It just takes time for it to sink in."

"I guess I'm still getting used to things." I twirled the stem of my glass between thumb and forefinger. The glass teetered, and I flattened my other hand over it, to keep it from toppling over. "I hate the lack of coordination."

"That might be the wine," she said.

It wasn't. I never tripped while I was a member of the undead society. *Almost* never. Okay, all the time, but I recovered pretty damn well. I gave her a half-shrug.

"How's Alex?" she asked.

The waiter approached with a bottle in hand, so I downed the rest of my wine and held my glass out for a refill. He poured another glass for Sheena and left us the bottle, saying the pizza would be right out.

"Alex is *fine*. He's ecstatic. And he's at work now, because *he* could get his job back," I said.

"*He* was only gone a few months. You were off the grid for years. And you can have another job."

She wasn't being very understanding or supportive. So much for having her in my corner. I sulked. "Like what?"

"Like becoming a partner in Sheena's Models. Silent partner. And you'd have to help with day-to-day operations, interviews, bookings—the whole shebang."

"Seriously?" My head was light, and she looked a little blurry. I squinted, to bring her to focus.

She guzzled her wine and added more. "Seriously. The vampettes scared Barbie away. You'll be doing me a favor."

Barbie was her latest assistant. I didn't like her much, but she loved her job and was good at it. The vampettes must have done something horrible, to make her quit.

"Okay. Yeah. When do I start?" *Hold on.* "No illegal, under-the-table crap this time, yes?"

In the past, Sheena maintained a second business in her ex-husband's name. What she did was organize the shooting of adult films starring her models, without her name showing, and without paying taxes for her cut. She'd booked me a couple projects, and ultimately *Knotting Cherry Stem*, for which I changed my name.

She shook her head like the thought never crossed her mind. "None of that. No shady stuff, and it'll all be down on paper. We'll draw a contract that says you're buying fifty percent of my company. Humans need paper trails. You'll need something to show the IRS."

How did other council members explain their never-depleting bank accounts? Where did council money come from? And were these questions a good enough reason for Constantine to take my call?

"We need to settle on a price," I said. "And a salary."

"We'll figure it all out. But first"—she tilted her head toward the waiter, who arrived with a huge pizza and hastily made room for it in the center of our table.

"Enjoy," he said.

Sheena cut a slice and brought it to her plate. I looked at the golden crust and the melted mozzarella rushing to fill in the gap left behind. The smell of pepperoni made my stomach rumble.

I took a slice too, hoping against hope that the taste would match the heavenly scents wafting from it.

It didn't.

Focus on the positive.

Human life. Incredible boyfriend. Now a job.

Would I trade any of it for tasty pizza?

Possibly. But only because I was hormonal.

Sheena insisted on buying, and I let her. The wine made me mellow and sleepy, and all I wanted was to go home, lose the tight jeans and high heels, and take a nap.

"I think you need to walk off the alcohol," Sheena said.

Bad Sheena, harshing my buzz. "Can't we call an Uber? The shoes are killing me."

"I'm parked three blocks from here. I'll drive you home. Wouldn't want Lover Boy to come after me for letting a stranger drive you home drunk."

Why would he care? "He doesn't care. He won't take my calls. And Wesley says not to give up, but I have to. Can't pine over him."

She frowned. "Over Al—? Oh. You mean Constantine."

"Don't say his name. He's out of my life." I covered both ears with my palms as we rounded the corner into an alley.

We were twenty feet from the main road, but it felt like a different city. No business people milling about. The cars looked older, the buildings more worn down.

I was too warm. I took off my blazer. I'd get a funny tan with the short sleeves, because now I could tan. I could do all sorts of things.

I didn't see where the man came from. I was tucking my blazer neatly around the handles of my Balenciaga, when he wrapped one arm around Sheena's waist and held his other fist out to me.

Something glinted in the early afternoon sun.

A blade. Too short to do much damage.

"Gimme the bag," the man told me.

I clutched it to my chest. Did the stupid human think he could come between me and my designer bag?

"Now, bitch." He looked over his shoulder. He seemed antsy.

Instead of offering a way out, my mind decided to absorb every little detail about our mugger. His beady eyes were red and puffy. He was missing his right upper lateral incisor. His shirt was filthy and strewn with burn holes, his arms full of tattoos, and he smelled rank. He shifted his weight from one foot to the other and sniffed. I looked into his eyes again. Feverish. In a moment of surprising clarity, I understood he was sick or high. I wouldn't feed on him if you paid me.

While Constantine and I were together, we spent an hour every evening sparring. He showed me mostly defensive moves, but also how to attack and feed from a human without causing lasting damage. It'd been a while since I last practiced, but I remembered most of it.

I went for the knife, feeling too slow. No. I didn't *feel* slow; I *was* slow. Human-slow. No longer supernatural. Stupid fuzzy brain.

The blade was sharp. It sliced through my forearm like a hot knife through butter. Blood pooled along the cut and then dripped on the fine leather.

I screamed.

The man grabbed Sheena's clutch, and then hugged her tight, before dropping her and running away.

"That was close," I whispered. My throat was tight again. So was my chest. The pizza and wine threatened to make a reappearance. "Let's go to your car. I'll call Alex, to meet us there."

Sheena didn't speak. She didn't move, either. She lay curled op on her side, where she fell.

Why did he hug her?

The blade.

Not a hug. A stab.

a series of muggings gone violent down town

Alex's case.

My knees buckled, and I welcomed the pain when they hit the sidewalk. I rolled Sheena on her back and saw a splotch of red spreading across her lilac jacket. Acid burned my throat, and a sour taste hit the roof of my mouth. I barely had time to turn away before emptying the contents of my stomach.

I wiped my mouth with the back of my hand, my head marginally clearer. Her chest rose and fell. Her skin had paled to a grayish hue, and her eyes were shut, but she moved her lips.

I pressed one palm on the side of her stomach, over the wound. Her blood seeping between my fingers reminded me of when Alex lay dying in his childhood bed, ripped bloody by Willoughby.

I'd saved Alex by sealing his wounds with my saliva and feeding him my blood.

I wasn't a vampire any longer. I couldn't heal Sheena with my blood or saliva. Couldn't fly her to the hospital.

I could only make a call and pray.

Chapter Fifteen

My fingers were slippery and sticky, and it took forever to find my phone and call up Constantine's cell on the touch screen.

I brought the phone to my ear. The ringing was interrupted by the *beep* that signified the battery was dying.

Fuck.

Pick up, pick up, pick up, I chanted in my head.

Sheena was still breathing. There was no blood coming out of her mouth. It was a good thing. Had to be. We'd save her. Constantine would save her.

"I'm sorry," I whispered, on the fourth ring. "I should have given him the stupid bag." Fresh tears ran down my cheeks.

"Not your fault, idiot." Her voice was barely audible and her eyes closed, but she was joking. We'd make it.

"Cherry, your persistence is doing neither of us any good." Constantine sounded sad more than annoyed.

"This is an emergency," I said. "Sheena was stabbed. I need you."

"Where are you?"

Beep. Battery.

I hurried to give him the street name and basic directions, and he said, "Don't move her. I'll be right there."

I tossed the phone in my purse and waited, watching Sheena's breathing.

It felt like an eternity before he flew in like a rocket and landed inches from Sheena and me. Without a glance my way, he knelt by her other side and lifted her shirt. A new bout of nausea made me avert my gaze. I couldn't watch him lick the wound closed.

Instead I went over the attack. God, I was stupid. I should have handed the mugger my bag. I could afford to replace it; I couldn't afford to lose Sheena. He could have killed us both. If I were a vampire, this wouldn't have happened. She wouldn't be in danger when she was with me. I'd be the predator, not the prey.

"The wound is deep," Constantine said. "If I close it on the outside, it may fester. I'll give her blood, to help her heal from the inside." He wouldn't meet my gaze, which gave me time to study him. Though the physical appearance of a vampire never changed, he looked haggard. His eyes seemed sunken, his cheeks hollow.

"What happened?" he asked.

"It was one man. He tried to get my bag. I thought I could disarm him," I mumbled.

"You obviously couldn't." He rolled up his sleeve, bit into his arm, and dripped blood into Sheena's mouth. She made a moue of distaste, but I saw her throat working a couple times. It should be enough.

"You're wounded too. I can smell it," Constantine said.

"It's nothing. Just a scrape." I held up my arm. Blood oozed to the surface but no longer dripped.

He flared his nostrils. "Smells different." He reached for my wrist and licked it clean. I felt the edges of the cut strain and the flesh bind together again. The sensation of his tongue on my skin sent a thrill down my spine and moisture pooling between my legs.

Not the right time. *So* not the right time.

"Constantine…" What could I say to make it all better between us?

He stood. "I've called for an ambulance. They should be here shortly. Sheena will be stable by then."

"Thank you," I said, as he turned away.

"I liked the red hair more," he said without looking back. When he reached the corner, he took off.

The ambulance showed up minutes later. Sheena had stopped bleeding. The EMTs cleaned and bandaged her cut, which was now only a flesh wound, and let me ride in the back with her.

Sheena seemed alert, but the painkillers she was administered en route apparently killed her brain-to-mouth filter, because she told the handsome Latino paramedic by her side that he had an amazing ass and could make hard cash as a stripper.

The paramedic laughed. "It's my second job, chica."

"*Sheena.*" I scowled at her, but all I felt was relief. She'd be okay. Thanks to Constantine.

As if she picked his name from my thoughts, she said, "Your ex is too hot for words. Bet I could make him famous, if he didn't have that immortality problem."

"She's a little loopy," I told the paramedic.

"It's the drugs. Don't worry about it."

Sheena snorted. "If I wasn't bleeding like a stuck pig when he raised my shirt, I'd show him a trick or two."

The man glanced at her stomach.

I beamed a smile at him. "Must be awesome drugs, huh?"

He gave a slow nod. "Better than I thought." A heartbeat later, he asked, "Where is the guy who called in the incident?"

"He came, he fed, he left her pining," Sheena muttered. Then she giggled. It was odd seeing her like this.

"He was a bystander. I think he chased our attacker," I said.

We didn't talk much till we reached the hospital. I expected the police to be waiting there for us to report the mugging, but the ambulance doors opened to reveal Liza's familiar face.

"Sheena said you're human now. Bummer," she told me with a wink, and then told our paramedic and the EMT driving that the women they'd picked up had nothing more serious than a case of food poisoning.

She also intervened when the hospital staff wouldn't let me know how Sheena was doing, and then thralled them to remember treating her for dehydration, not blood loss.

Sheena got a suite with round-the-clock care. Liza arranged everything, while I watched from the sidelines.

I cleaned up as well as I could and sat by Sheena's bed to hold her hand, while she drifted off for the tenth time after more lewd remarks about Constantine and his tongue.

Liza came to the room and pulled up a chair next to mine. "All done. No record of the attack. Constantine asked me and the girls to find the guy for him, but I said I'd ask what you want to do."

"I think it's Alex's case. He'll want to be involved."

She nodded. "Is he at the scene now?"

Shit-crap-fuck. "I haven't called him yet." Because I forgot all about him.

Though really, my best friend lay bleeding on the street. A vampire had a better chance of helping than a cop did. I was right to call Constantine first.

But I didn't call Alex second. Or at all.

I fished for my phone in my bag. The screen was still smudged. I used a wipe with disinfectant to clean it, but I couldn't call him. The phone was out of juice. It was as good an excuse as any to put off a discussion I didn't want to have.

A male nurse came in to shoo me off near sundown. Visiting hours were over.

I looked at Liza, expecting her to work her vampire mojo, but she shook her head. "I'll stay the night. You need to go home. Get some rest. Come back in the morning."

"Yeah, you look like shit," Sheena croaked.

I flipped her the bird, but it was with love. She and Liza were right. I needed rest and a hot shower. And to stop thinking of how Constantine rushed to Sheena's rescue but didn't spare me a glance. And of how his dismissal cut deeper than our mugger's blade.

Why couldn't I forget about Constantine? He was my past, and a rocky one at that.

Alex was my future.

And he was naked when he opened the door and pulled me inside the house. Our house. "Ta *dah*," he said with flourish. Then he got a better look at me. "What the fuck? What happened? Are you okay?"

"Yes. I'm fine." I motioned at the blood soaking my T-shirt. "Not mine. Sheena and I went for lunch. As we were leaving, a guy went for my purse. I tried to stop him, and he stabbed her." My voice broke. "It was all my fault."

More tears? I should be dehydrated by now.

Alex gathered me in his arms and kissed the top of my head. "Shhh, baby. It's all right. You're okay. Is Sheena...?"

I may have wiped snot on his bare chest. Disgusting, I know, but it's the human condition. Suck it up. "She's in the hospital. Constantine managed to save her life, but she needed stitches and they're keeping her for a couple days, to monitor her."

"Constantine was there? I thought he didn't want to see you again." He didn't sound upset, but he had mad interrogating skills and a crazy-good poker face.

I didn't try to hide the truth. "She was losing too much blood to make it to the hospital. I called him because he could make that stop." I looked into Alex's eyes, so he'd read the truth in mine. I didn't choose Constantine over him; I simply thought of Constantine first because he was the best man for the specific job.

"Did you call the police?" Alex asked.

"No. We didn't know how to explain that Sheena was already healing. I think the guy who did it might be the one you're looking for. He had nothing to gain by stabbing her, but he did anyway. It made no sense, Alex. Does human life matter so little?"

He hesitated, then said, "You drank human blood till a couple days ago."

"But I didn't kill them. I don't get how someone would do this for a few bucks."

He pulled me close again and tucked my head under his chin. His hard body supported and anchored me. "It's one of the things I love about you. Despite your choices, despite the porn, despite everything, you're a good, decent person inside."

His words were meant as praise, but they were a misogynist load of crap. I was too tired to point out that there was no *despite* here. My choices made me.

Alex was a good man. He didn't realize he insulted me. I'd talk to him about it in the morning.

"Go wash off the grime," he said. "I've made pasta. We'll eat, and you'll tell me about your attacker."

"Okay."

His priorities were right. This was what he needed to know. But when I plugged my phone to the charger and saw no missed calls from him, it pissed me off that he hadn't cared to ask about my job interview.

I was being irrational. Irritable. But last time I brushed off my worries and made excuses for him, he went psycho on me.

As the too-hot—no, too-cold… wait, too hot again—water soaked my head and ran down my body to form pale red rivulets beneath my feet, I went over Alex's behavior the past couple days. No red flags. No irrational jealousy. No outbursts. Maybe he saw certain things a different way than I did. That was to be expected. With time, our ragged edges would grind against one another and smoothen out until we fit together comfortably.

'Cause that was what solid human relationships became, once bodies aged and passion faded. Comfortable.

Thirty was too young for me to be thinking like this. I was okay. Sheena was okay. I had a job. I had Alex.

Mentally repeating the reminder as a mantra was soothing.

The void inside mocked me. I had to woman up and face it, instead of sidestepping along its ledge. I missed Constantine. I hadn't been ready to lose him. Having him inside me again after all this time had brought to the surface feelings I'd done a great job of ignoring for a long while. I knew I loved him when I agreed to give him up, but I didn't expect it to hurt this much, like part of me was stolen. Like a weight pressed on my heart with every breath.

It didn't change the facts. I was human, and I was with Alex. Constantine wanted nothing to do with me. Besides, even if I hadn't chosen humanity, there was no happily-ever-after that involved all three of us.

The pasta was creamy and cheesy and filling, but it didn't help me feel better. My sense of taste remained suppressed, and hearing Alex's delighted moan at the first bite of bacon, chicken, and parm linguini only made me gloomier.

I described our attacker, surprised at the effort it took to recall details I knew I'd noticed.

Alex asked questions from time to time. He told me how brave I was for fighting back. That I thought clearly under pressure and my actions saved my friend's life. That he loved me.

He cupped my cheek, and I leaned into his touch. "I love you too," I said.

It would have to be enough.

Chapter Sixteen

I was back by Sheena's bedside bright and early the next morning. Liza spent the night here, as she promised. I secretly envied the spryness in her step when she stood to greet me. If I spent last night in a chair, I'd need a spa day to loosen my muscles this morning.

"She's still asleep," Liza said. "I think it's more her lifestyle catching up to her than the knife wound. She hasn't been sleeping much these days, with… work." Before I could ask what it was about work that kept Sheena up at night, Liza added, "I fed her more blood, and she's mostly healed. She should be able to go home when she wakes up."

I hugged her and held on despite her stiff posture. "Thank you. I don't know what we'd do if it weren't for Constantine and you."

"No problem. Constantine found her purse nearby. Seemed like only cash and credit cards were missing."

I opened my mouth to speak, but Liza said, "He already arranged for her cards to be cancelled. Sally will get Sheena's car and come by in a few hours. She'll help you check Sheena out without questions."

God, I was a horrible friend. I didn't think of any of the practical stuff. I thanked her again, took her place in the uncomfortable chair, and waited.

Sheena's eyes moved under her closed lids. Her chest rose and fell with unhindered, long breaths. Nurses checked her pulse and temperature, then *mmmed* approvingly. She was okay, no thanks to me.

It was around noon, and I was dozing off, when Sheena whispered, "Hope you brought me a donut." She had one eye open.

I laughed and squeezed her hand. "I'll buy you a dozen when we're out of here."

She opened her second eye, sat up, and patted her hair, which was a fluffy dark cloud around her head. "Who messed with the hair?"

"They checked you for a concussion last night. The bun got in the way. You're lucky Liza didn't let them shave you."

She grumbled. I handed her a hairband and watched her tame her frizzy mane into submission.

"When can we leave?" she asked.

"As soon as Sally gets here."

As if I conjured her, Sally stepped in the room. With her hair pulled back in a ponytail, she looked like a teenager.

"Were you waiting outside till someone called your name?" Sheena sounded cheerful. As if she hadn't had a near-death experience. Maybe Liza helped with that.

"Huh?" Sally said.

I had the feeling it didn't take much to confuse her, but she was a sweetheart. "Will you get a doctor to sign off on Sheena's release?" I asked.

"I did you one better." Sally bounced on her toes, a grin threatening to slice her face in half. "No staff members remember you being here. Let's go." For someone who weeks ago would rather kill herself than remain a vampire, she certainly enjoyed her mind-control abilities.

We helped Sheena get dressed in a clean change of clothes Sally brought—why didn't I think of that?—and the three of us exited the hospital with no trouble whatsoever.

"I parked over there." Sally pointed to Sheena's car right outside the sliding doors. "And don't yell, but I cancelled your appointments for Monday and Tuesday. You need to take it easy. You could have died."

Sheena gave her a death glare, but all she said was, "I'm fine."

"Are you sure?" I asked. "You didn't even threaten to mop the floor with her ass."

"I'm too hungry to be throwing around threats, but I'm pain free and well rested. I don't think I've slept this well in ages."

Lucky her.

Sally drove, despite Sheena's protests. We got donuts on the way, and I called Alex and let him know Sally and I would be taking Sheena home and spending the day with her.

At Sheena's, I made us a salad, which we proceeded to ignore in favor of the donuts.

Sally offered to do our nails "—since I can't do my own." She looked so crestfallen as she looked at her perma-nude fingernails, I let her do mine, though I paid for a manicure three days ago.

"You know, Cherry will be working with me now on," Sheena said, washing down her bite with a glass of Chianti.

I glared. "Should you be drinking that?"

"Liza said my liver's as good a new. I have to break it in."

Sally giggled, then sobered up. "So Barbie isn't coming back?"

Sheena looked at the glass she held, then the rest of the donut in her other hand. Then she dunked the donut in the wine and bit into it. "Doubtful." To me, she said, "All three of them vamped out when she accidentally stapled her finger. You should've seen them. They were offering first aid, fangs out. Barbie flew out the door and emailed me her resignation the same evening. Poor thing."

"Poor thing," Sally echoed, but she was giggling again.

I loved the time with the two of them, and things only got better when Liza and Carrie came home with tacos. I was shocked when the first bite tasted like heaven, and wolfed down three of them before pacing myself with the fourth. It seemed my sense of taste was returning. Good day, all around.

The girls and I were discussing work—jobs the vampettes wanted to book, new clients Sheena hoped to woo, time schedules and days off for me—when Alex called. He wanted to drop by and see the girls, since he hadn't spoken to them in a while. I saw the young vampires exchange uncertain looks, so I told him Sheena was tired and I was about to go home anyway.

"What was that about?" I asked when I hung up.

"What?" Carrie slathered sour cream on her taco, looking all too innocent.

"The looks. Do you have a problem with Alex?"

Liza shook her head. "No. No problem."

"Good, because he died saving your undead asses."

Sally turned her gaze to the floor. "Alex is great, but we don't like what he did to you."

"And we're worried he might do it again," Liza added.

"And Const—" Whatever Sally was about to say was hushed by the three others.

"What about him?" My voice sounded louder than I was going for.

"Nothing," Sheena said. "He's fine. We're all fine. You and Alex should drop by for dinner sometime this week."

I narrowed my eyes. "What aren't you telling me?"

"Nothing."

I looked at the vampires. "Nothing?"

They shook their heads. Sally avoided my gaze. I'd get to the bottom of this, but not now.

"I should be going," I said.

Sheena offered to give me a ride to work on Monday. Carrie said she'd drop by. See how things were. She and Sheena exchanged another of those weird looks. Hmm…

I called a cab. I should buy a car. Or maybe Alex could drive me to work every morning. Nah. I'd get a car. Maybe a driver too.

The evening got chilly while I waited outside. I regretted not taking a jacket with this morning—not that I planned to be out all day. I hugged myself. Days ago, this would be the perfect temperature.

Days ago, everything was different.

Tonight, Alex was waiting for me at home.

The cab driver wasn't chatty, which left me alone with my thoughts. I had way too much time to myself lately. Work would fix that. Work and focusing on Alex. On being his girlfriend. His return to his human life was seamless. If I took my cues from him and tried to be normal, maybe it'd come back to me, like my taste did.

The door was unlocked, so I let myself in. Alex was cooking. He had on his mother's apron, and I smiled at the memory of the first time I saw him wear it. He'd been naked underneath. Now he wore his jeans and a T-shirt that hugged his broad shoulders as he chopped lettuce.

"Hey you," he said, without raising his gaze. "Hungry? I was going for a Caesar's, but there's no bacon."

I leaned my hip on the table behind him. "I've eaten, and it's always a *no* to no bacon."

He washed his hands, patted them dry on a dishtowel hanging from the glass cupboard, and gave me a light kiss on the corner of my lips. "How's Sheena?"

"She ate her weight in donuts and didn't keel over, so I guess she's fine." I laughed, but I felt so very tired, all of a sudden.

He got a roasted chicken fillet from the fridge and began slicing it. "We have a suspect for the muggings. We put out an APB, but nothing yet. Roebuck wouldn't let me sign out his file, but if you drop by the precinct tomorrow or Monday, you can go over some mug shots."

"Monday, I guess. Maybe after work."

He abandoned the chicken and faced me again. "Work? The meeting yesterday went well? I meant to ask, but with everything that happened…"

He didn't know anything happened till I got home last night. He could have asked. And I was being selfish. Yesterday was his first day back to work. I didn't ask how that went, either.

"The meeting was horrible, but Sheena offered me half of her agency. We'll be partners." I grinned, and so did he. This was normal.

"That's awesome. We should celebrate. Screw the salad—we're going out." He pulled me toward the door, but I planted my feet on the ground.

"I'm tired. Maybe tomorrow? Or your next day off?"

He brought my hand to his lips and kissed my knuckles. The gesture reminded me of Constantine.

I pulled away as soon as I could without making it seem like I hated his touch. "Any news on Ruby? I didn't ask her when she's leaving again."

Alex returned to preparing his dinner. "She called this morning. She's back in Romania."

"That was fast. Thought she'd want to stay a little longer." Maybe visit her old friend Constantine.

"We came back on Tuesday so"—he counted days on his fingers—"that's four days. Huh. I thought it was longer. Anyway, she was in a hurry to return to Europe."

But I was stuck on the first part of his answer. "You flew in together? How come she didn't come to the mansion with you?"

Alex shook his head. "Ruby doesn't do commercial flights. She used Constantine's jet and landed here a few hours later. It needed to refuel and go through security checks, and I couldn't wait that long."

Aw, he'd been in a hurry to come home to me.

"Ruby dropped by your parents'. They didn't mention anything about your… reversal, so she didn't say anything, but she said you should call them."

"I wanted to tell them up close. Maybe next weekend."

"Gerri"—there was my real name again, not the one he met me under, because I was no longer that person to him—"you're human. Don't you think they'd like to know as soon as possible? I mean, they can be grandparents now."

I was lightheaded. It felt a lot like blood loss. Had to be my period. "I'll call them. Tomorrow."

Salad ready, he asked once more if I wanted some, and when I said no, sat at the table while I pulled out a chair across from him.

I should change out of the clothes I wore all day. I felt heat more intensely when I was undead, but I didn't sweat back then. I kicked off my ballet pumps and wiggled my toes. Freedom. I sat there, listening to Alex go on about his day and work and how happy the guys at the precinct were to see him, while I itched to get out of my clothes and have a shower. If flavors were returning to what they used to be, I might finally get used to the water jet.

I escaped upstairs as soon as Alex put the last bit of lettuce in his mouth, and only went back down once I was squeaky clean and in shorts and a tank top. I drifted off on the couch and woke up in bed the next morning, in the same clothes.

I didn't change out of them on Sunday, most of which Alex and I spent online shopping. After hours in front of his laptop, we bought a state-of-the-art widescreen TV, a new double bed with a memory foam mattress, and finally—to Alex's utter horror and despite his numerable protests—a car for me.

While I didn't mind splurging on other things, in this case, I went with a used Toyota Prius. My driving skills were rusty, and I didn't trust myself with anything bigger, faster, or more expensive. I did pay a little extra, to have it delivered to our doorstep Monday afternoon.

Chapter Seventeen

Sheena drove me to the station before work, to unofficially identify the guy who stabbed her. She waited in the car; she hadn't seen enough of him to recognize his picture. Alex was swamped, so we didn't talk much. I basically pointed to the right pic, said I'd be home for dinner, and blew him a kiss.

Sheena stopped for smoothies on the way to the office. I watched her for signs of discomfort as she exited and reentered the car, and I was happy to see no stiffness in her movements. She really was fine—physically, at least.

"They give potential clients a good example," she said, as she handed me a kale-something mixture. She placed hers in the driver's side cup holder.

I took a sip and wished my sense of taste was still numb. "Yuck."

"I didn't say you should drink it. Carry it around. Maybe swirl the straw while you interview someone." She wasn't all the way back to her usual color combinations, but the fuchsia button-down shirt she wore with her black slacks was a step in that direction.

"I'm gonna need coffee," I said.

"Just keep it in your drawer. We're supposed to be all about healthy living."

As we pulled into traffic again, I flashed back to the chocolate-glazed fried bites of sin we indulged in on Saturday. "Since when?"

"Since Sally suggested that as our new pitch. Everyone has thin models, but with the rise of the clean-living movement, we can provide companies with people who take care of themselves."

"People? We're taking on men now too?"

"We're more inclusive, in general."

"Is that also Sally's idea?"

Sheena nodded. "The girl is a marketing genius."

"Or she hopes to meet hot guys," I said with a smirk.

Sheena laughed. "Then she's an evil genius."

We parked in an above-ground parking garage and walked a couple of blocks. The building entrance was open. I went in first, and called the elevator.

"Not that way." Sheena grabbed my elbow, almost making me spill my kale-flavored vileness—and wouldn't that be a crying shame?—and led me toward the stairs. "It's only three flights."

Come. Fucking. On.

By the third floor landing, my thighs burned with exertion. I needed to work out more. Or at all.

Sheena moved to unlock the door, while I studied the Sheena's Models sign.

"Will my name go up there too?" I asked.

"Sure. Who doesn't want to be signed up by Gertrude Mosby? No, you won't go up there, doofus." She flicked my ear and led the way in. "This is your desk."

"I know my way around. Thanks." It used to be Barbie's desk. "And I know what's in here." I opened the top drawer, expecting to see the huge-ass folder Barbie kept client info in, but nada.

Sheena crossed her arms over her chest and gave me her best you-don't-know-shit look. "We've gone fully electronic. It's planet-friendly. You'll be lucky to find a pack of Post-It notes in the entire office."

O... kay. "Sally's idea?"

"Nope. Carrie digitalized everything. I'll ask her to show you when she gets here, because I don't know my way around her system yet."

Sheena disappeared into the small kitchenette. When she returned, she jingled two keys in her hand. "For you. Main entrance and front door." She tossed them at me, and I reached for them, but I missed and they hit my smoothie, which sloshed all over my desk.

"You did that on purpose." Sheena arched an eyebrow.

I shook my head. "But I'm not gonna mourn its loss."

I cleaned the green goop from my desk and the floor, and by the time I was properly caffeinated, Carrie showed up.

"Everything okay?" Sheena asked her, as she let her in.

Carrie gave a quick shake of the head I supposed I wasn't meant to see, and then said, "Why wouldn't it be?"

"No reason. Never mind me. Been on edge since the mugging."

No, she wasn't. With the exception of her outfits, she seemed like her usual self.

I planted my fists on my hips. "Oh, come on. Tell me what's wrong."

They looked at each other, then back at me. "Constantine doesn't want you involved," Carrie said.

My very being protested that sentence. I shouldn't be involved, but Sheena was?

Then again, Sheena hadn't hurt him...

"Okay. But if he's in any danger, you let me know," I said to Carrie.

"I will."

I studied her. I was used to seeing her around the house and had stopped being amazed at how beautiful she was. In her ripped jeans, tight tank top, and ballet flats, with her long brown hair falling down her shoulders and her makeup expertly applied, she looked a hundred percent the swimsuit model she was—the woman Willoughby killed and recruited to his and Ádísa's army of gorgeous undead killers.

And she was apparently a computer whiz.

She spent a couple hours showing me her filing system and the online backup she kept, on *the cloud*, and I pretended to understand everything.

When she asked, "Got it?" I nodded.

"I'll call you if I have any questions." I'd better add her number to speed-dial.

The doorbell rang, and Carrie pulled up the schedule on the list. "I think it's your first walk-in."

Sheena rushed to her glass-walled office and closed the door behind her. I buzzed in the newcomer and steepled my fingers, trying to look like I knew what I was doing. Inside, I berated myself for feeling jittery. But think about it—I hadn't had a job in half a dozen years. Never had a *desk* job before that.

A tall, ethereal blonde stepped inside. She marched to my desk on impossibly long legs, hugging a folder to her chest. "Good morning. I'm Cecilia Torrent, and I want to become a model." Her smile was dazzling.

I kept my expression professional. "Do you have an appointment?"

The corners of her lips wobbled, before her expression turned upbeat again. "I do not. I was hoping Ms. Herring would see me today. I'm only in town for a few hours."

And she hadn't thought to call ahead. I knew the system. Act like the agent is intruding on your time.

I liked Cecilia Torrent's attitude.

"I'll see if she'll fit you in." I let myself in Sheena's office and whispered, "She's gorgeous. Has the right style. Nothing overdone. She's like a sexy blonde gazelle."

Sheena replied in the same tone, "Have her wait. Maybe next time she'll make an appointment."

I returned to my desk, sat, and looked up at her. "Please take a seat." I motioned to the waiting area.

"Thank you so much." Her smile grew wider, and I couldn't keep from returning it this time.

"You didn't get her info," Carrie whispered from behind me.

Shit. "I'll do it when she's on the way out."

"You're supposed to log all meetings."

"I will. After she leaves." I bit out the words.

"Okay. Maybe offer her something to drink?"

"Maybe stop backseat driving?"

Carrie relented, and I opened a new file for Cecilia, with just her name for now.

I rocked the shit out of Candy Crush Soda on my phone, until Sheena told me to send Cecilia in.

Fifteen, then twenty minutes ticked by, and she wasn't coming back out. Good for her. Sheena weighed people at a glance, and for her to still be talking to Cecilia, it was good news.

The skip in Cecilia's step when she returned to my desk confirmed it. She started to speak, when the phone rang. I held up a finger for her to wait.

"Make an appointment for her with Jade this afternoon," Sheena said over the line. New hairdo, and with

Sheena's own stylist. "Then call Trent. I need new portfolio pics tomorrow. If he's a diva about it, remind him he owes me."

This Trent guy was her new photographer, then. Carrie called up *Associates* on the screen and scrolled down to his number. This electronic filing was cool.

"Yes, Ms. Herring." I hung up and turned to Cecilia. "I thought you were only in town for a few hours."

She blushed and lowered her head. "I'm sorry. I really wanted to see Ms. Herring, and when I called on Friday I was told I'd have to wait a month for an appointment."

She must have talked to Sally.

I asked for her info, and she was more than forthcoming with the details. She was born and raised in L.A. Always wanted to be a model, but her parents wouldn't let her until she graduated high school. She just moved in with her boyfriend, and she was eighteen. Twelve years younger than me.

I felt old.

I booked Cecilia an appointment, convinced Trent—who sounded friendly once I mentioned Sheena—to meet her at his studio at seven in the morning, and sent her on her merry way.

Then I called Dr. King again. And was told there were still no openings.

Carrie checked her phone and grimaced. "It's almost two."

"If you need to go, go. I'm good for now. I'll call you if I need help." *If.* Ha.

"I'll wait for Sally to get here first."

Huh. "Have you left Sheena's side since Friday?" I asked.

"I wasn't with her on Friday," she said.

"But Liza was. And then Sally on Saturday. Is there a reason you're guarding her round the clock?"

Carrie huffed. "You weren't supposed to know, but we worry about you."

Not Sheena? "Me? Why?"

"Because all this is new, and you may need time to process, and something may happen while you're processing."

"Like what?"

"Like get mugged again. I don't know. We worry. You, Sheena, and Wesley are our human family now—Alex too, but more like a distant cousin—and we wanna keep you around."

This gorgeous vampire would *not* make me cry.

I hugged her. "I'm okay."

"Well, good," she said stiffly, "but we'll still check from time to time."

Sally let herself in, chirping about a guy who flirted with her on the way here. "He was *so* hot. Like *oh my God* hot."

Emotional moment diffused.

Carrie left, and Sally and I ordered something to eat. It was a salad, but I felt every single flavor. *Win.* Sheena joined us, and then said we could call it a day.

"Can we make a detour on the way home?" I asked her.

"Sure. What for?"

"Upgrades." To Sally I said, "I need your help with something."

She widened her eyes. "What is it? It won't get me in trouble with Constantine, will it?"

Hearing his name was no easier than uttering it. It twisted my insides. I needed a distraction. Needed to do something for me. And Sally could… facilitate that.

"I need you to get me a doctor's appointment ASAP," I said.

"Oh no. Are you sick? Please say you're not dying." Tears welled in her eyes.

This goes to show everyone that vampires aren't monsters, by the way.

I hurried to reassure her. "I'm fine. It's a plastic surgeon. Being a human takes a toll on the body, and I want to firm some things up. Maybe enlarge others?"

"Oh." She looked me over and nodded, like she recognized the problem areas. "I can do that. We'll have you looking thirty again in no time."

Grumble grumble.

We locked up, and I found Dr. King's address while we got the car. Maybe I'd ask for a facelift too.

* * * *

I was relieved when Dr. King didn't remember me. Of course he saw thousands of patients every year, but I took the lack of recognition in his gaze as extra confirmation that my makeover worked.

Sheena waited in the car, while Sally used her vampire gaze to book me a breast augmentation—despite my efforts, the doctor wouldn't call it a boob job—and liposuction for Monday after next. Sally promised to assist with the healing, bless her. In two weeks, I'd have the body I always wanted. Though Dr. King mentioned collagen depletion and crow's feet more than once, I wouldn't have him work on my face. I'd invest in a good day cream instead. Okay, and possibly get fillers around the eyes.

Chapter Eighteen

As Sheena swerved into our street, I saw a sight that made me squeal. A silver Prius sat in our driveway.

Sheena pulled up behind it, and I flew—well, not really, because I couldn't do that now—out of the back seat.

"Do you like my new ride?" I hovered my palm over the roof, and felt the heat of the day reflected back at me.

Sally cheered from the passenger seat, while Sheena gave me a thumbs-up. "Goes with our new brand too."

I laughed. "That's a happy coincidence. But it's here early."

A sound came from behind, and I turned startled toward the house, to see Alex walking out the door. "They needed someone to sign for the delivery, and called me. You must have given them the wrong number."

"Sorry I made you leave work."

"It's okay. Had to pick up something else too. These are the temporary plates. Guy said you need to go sort out the paperwork and get the final ones in a week." He came down the porch stairs to give me a kiss, and then continued toward the girls.

I felt a tightening in my chest that loosened when they both got out of the car and gave him hugs and pecks on the cheek.

"Are you coming inside? I can make coffee. I have an hour before I go back in," Alex said.

Sheena and Sally thanked him for the offer but declined.

"Where are the keys? I'm taking you out for coffee," I said once they were gone. "I'll drop you off at work after."

He fished a key fob out of his pocket and dangled it in the air as he approached me. I snatched it and unlocked the car, but Alex stopped me before I reached for the door handle.

"I have something for you too." He produced a small velvet box from his other pocket.

And I froze.

I don't mean I couldn't move; an icy hand ran down my spine, and the numbness spread to my limbs. I tried to smile. My chest felt tight, my heart slammed against my ribs, and my stupid lungs refused to let air in.

Was he going to propose?

I zeroed in on his hand raising the lid of the box, and the image slowed. Flickered. Broke. Like I was watching an old film reel.

What would I say if he did? He'd mentioned getting engaged, but this was too soon. Way too soon. He sometimes left dirty dishes in the sink and forgot to take out the trash and talked during movies and—

Was I hyperventilating?

I was hyperventilating.

I had to stop him from opening the box, but no words came out of my mouth and I couldn't raise my hand to place it over his. Was this what a heart attack felt like? Nah. It was just cold feet. Right?

I couldn't say *yes*. Would *no* mean we were breaking up? Should I accept and then stall?

No. No no no no no.

We were back together less than a week. Too soon. We didn't know if we were compatible. We'd been together longer as vampires, but the circumstances were different.

He opened the box. The box was open.

Oh thank fuck.

There was something shiny in it, but it wasn't a ring. I gulped in air and willed my heartrate to return to normal. "A key?" I smiled with relief. "It's a key for the house."

"It was about time you had your own." Alex held it out to me. The keyring was a bejeweled *G*. For *Gerri*.

I took it with shaking hands and burrowed in Alex's arms. "Thank you." The pressure in my chest was lighter but still there.

He kissed the crown of my head. "You're very welcome, but this is your place too."

I pulled him down for a deep kiss that soothed my nerves more. "It's Key-Day for Cherry," I said when we broke apart. "Got a set for the agency too."

"Sounds like a day for celebration." He winked.

"French press and handmade crostini will have to do for now, but I'll get a bottle of wine for tonight, and maybe we can…" I waggled my eyebrows.

He glanced beneath my waist. "So we're—"

"Cleared for landing."

"Wanna skip coffee?"

"Tempting, but I want to take this baby for a ride." I tilted my head toward the car.

He gave an exaggerated roll of the eyes. "If you haffta."

I slid in behind the wheel and adjusted the seat and the mirrors while Alex got in next to me.

Now, I'm the first to admit I reversed a little faster than I should have, but there was no reason for him to yell. I didn't hit anything, and the rest of the drive was smooth. Parking took a couple more tries than I'd like, but it was all coming back to me fast, which did wonders for my mood.

Until we were seated at the brasserie, and Alex asked, "Why did you freak out earlier?"

"Earlier?" I hid behind my menu.

"When you thought there was a ring in that box." Alex took the plasticized card from me. "I'm a cop; I'm good at reading body language. Though I didn't need my training in this case. You were like a deer caught in the headlights."

"I was surprised."

The waiter came for our order, and Alex asked for more time, before returning to me. "You were terrified."

I gulped. "It's too soon, Alex." Possibly for everything.

He nodded. "Which is why I wasn't proposing. But you're open to the idea in the future." He said it as a statement, but it was a question.

Saying I was would be the end of it, and we could enjoy our afternoon till he had to return to work, but I didn't want to lie. "Maybe?"

"Are you asking *me*?"

"I don't know, Alex. I love you. I'm sure about that. But I don't see me getting married or having kids anytime soon. My priorities are different right now." My phone rang, and I pulled it out to see Dr. King's number flashing on the screen. "Sorry. I have to get this," I said.

It was the doctor's assistant, to confirm the date for the procedure and give me instructions not to eat or drink for hours beforehand.

I asked Alex for his pen and a page of the little notebook he always carried about, and jotted everything down.

When I ended the call, he was looking at me, brow furrowed.

Shit. I should have told him. "I'm getting cosmetic surgery in two weeks. I only booked it today. Literally just before I got home. Sally *convinced* the guy to see me when his assistant was out, so she called for the details."

"I didn't know you were considering it."

"Sure you did." I tried to sound playful, hoping to diffuse the situation. "I told you in the car, when I saw myself in the mirror."

"I thought you were joking." He clenched his jaw. So much for diffusing the situation. "I was kidding about the wrinkles. You know that."

I waved him off. "Not touching the face, but I've always wanted a slimmer waist and maybe something more on the cleavage area."

He pointed a finger at me. "You're beautiful the way you are, Gerri. Belly and all. You have nothing to prove."

I loved the part about being beautiful. The assumption that I'd alter my body to *prove* something, not so much. "I'm doing this for me," I said slowly. "It's my body."

"I know it is, but you want to change it because you think it'll make you more attractive. Do you realize you won't be able to get pregnant for the next three or four years? What'll you tell your parents and my mom when they ask why we're waiting?"

Lipo isn't a tummy tuck. They don't tighten your muscles, and you don't have to wait years to get pregnant, but that wasn't the point. "I wasn't planning on getting knocked up anytime soon, and I don't generally base my decisions on how I'll explain them to others." My eyes burned. I wanted to be a vampire for ten seconds, so I could thrall this discussion to an end.

He glared. "You obviously don't care what *others* have to say, but it's not all about you anymore. You can't do anything you please and damn the consequences. And when will you want to have kids? Neither of us is getting any younger."

You know how sometimes you can't tell the moment a relationship died? Well, that was when I realized ours had run its course, and it wasn't 'cause of his jibe about my age.

What I felt when I saw him with the box wasn't cold feet. It was a fucking full-on panic attack, and I felt it resurging inside, clouding my reason. My first instinct was to pick a fight—tell Alex I didn't care about his opinion and he wouldn't see the new boobs anyway, because we were over. But I wasn't pissed off; I was sad. And Alex was the one who taught me not to translate all my feelings into anger just because it was easier to handle.

I threw the approaching waiter a death-glare that kept him at bay. "Alex, this isn't working. *We* are not working." The words burned my lips, but I didn't want to take them back. Whether things between us were more broken than I thought when we got back together, or we simply weren't at the same place, this wasn't working.

"Because we're disagreeing on liposuction?"

"It's not this disagreement." Hell, when I thought about it, I didn't want the lipo anymore. I was no longer the girl who considered her value to be reversely proportional to the circumference of her waist. Becoming human again had confused me for a while, but I saw clearly now. The boobs I very much wanted, though. For me. Not to be more attractive.

I made a fist, digging my nails in my palm to keep from screaming. "When we met, I thought we couldn't have a future because I was a vampire. Then you got turned, and the problem was that you weren't used to your new reality. I believed with both of us human, we'd be good, but I was wrong. You want a serious girlfriend, someone you can marry, and I'm not that girl."

He cupped my fist with both hands. "But you can be. If you're set on doing this, let's talk about it."

I squeezed more tightly. There was nothing to talk about. "You're not listening. I'm saying I don't want to be the perfect woman you have in your head. I'm not ready for all this relationship entails, and I don't know if I'll ever—"

Alex glanced at the ceiling. When he zeroed in on me again, his expression was flat. "This is about Constantine, isn't it?"

I withdrew from his grip so fast, I hit my hand on the wall. It hurt. "This is about you and me," I whispered, frustration and pain choking me. Anything else, we could overcome, but we weren't compatible in our core. "We're not meant to be, Alex. I don't want the picket fence and the family you always dreamed of." Realization dawned, and I added, "Not now, not ever."

"Gerri, I love you. We can work this out." He didn't say he didn't care about anything but me.

"I love you too, but we'll never see eye to eye, and this isn't fixable." I stood.

Alex got up to block my way. He reached for me but didn't touch me. "Come home with me. Stay the night." His steel-grey eyes were mesmerizing, and I wanted to say *yes*.

It was tempting. I really did love him, and I'd never *not* be attracted to him, but another night together would only prolong our misery.

I leaned into him and pressed my lips to his. He tasted salty with the tears that ran down my cheeks. I handed him the key fob. "I'll call Sheena to pick me up. Take my car to work. I'll come pick it up and get my stuff tomorrow morning, and I'll leave the house key."

Leaving him behind looking like a lost pup hurt like hell, but I also felt liberated. No Constantine. No Alex. Just me, and time to figure out who I was and what I wanted.

I called Sheena and got a vampire lift to her place.

Chapter Nineteen

"And you don't think you can patch things up?" Sally scrunched her adorable nose, as we landed at Sheena's front door.

"No. It's over." I sniffled, though I'd exhausted my sobs on the flight here.

"It's normal for a guy to want to be consulted when his girl is about to make a major change," she said in a soft tone. "Haven't met one who'd make a fuss over extra boobage, though."

I'd glossed over the details when she picked me up, and I didn't have the will or the stamina to explain now. "Can we talk in the morning?"

"Sure." Still, she looked at me eagerly.

"What?"

"Nothing."

Nothing, my ass, but I didn't care to find out what she wanted to say. I pointed at the door. "Do you have a key, or do I ring the bell or knock or something?"

"Does this mean you'll become a vampire again?" Sally asked.

We weren't done, then.

"I just need to be alone for a while." I rang the doorbell anyway, praying someone on the other side of the door would save me.

"You could call Constantine. He's alone too." Sally grinned.

I groaned and knocked on the door. "Sheena? Somebody? Anybody?"

Sheena opened the door, and I rushed past her into the living room, away from Sally's questions. Not that I escaped her.

"It wasn't just a fight," Sally told the room. "They broke up."

Liza got up from the couch. "I'll get wine."

Carrie ran in the kitchen after her. "I'm making snacks."

Sally sort of tackled me to the couch and wrapped a throw around my shoulders. "Get comfy and tell us all about it."

I shrugged it off. "It's a million degrees."

She pouted and started to say something, but Sheena wedged herself between us and sat next to me. "What does the situation call for? Do we go with *poor you, you can do better*, or *I never liked him anyway*?"

I thought I was cried out, but Sheena's question brought on a fresh bout.

"Now look what you've done," Sally stage whispered.

"It was meant to be a joke," Sheena said. "I swear, if that boy did anything to hurt you again, I'll feed his balls to my dog."

"You don't have a dog," I managed between sniffles.

"I'll buy one if I have to. Do I have to?"

I shook my head. "He didn't do anything."

Liza returned, holding a bottle of white in one hand and a tray with glasses on the other. "You're not covering for him, are you? I know abusers—"

"*Alex is not an abuser*." I slapped the arm of the couch. The *oof* at impact was unsatisfying. "He's back to his sweet self, and he wants us to get married and have kids. And I don't."

"He couldn't wait?" Carrie asked, placing a platter of sandwiches on the coffee table. She took a throw pillow, put it on the floor, and sat on it cross legged. "Men."

I slumped back and closed my eyes. "No reason for him to wait. I thought, if I were human, I'd want the same things. I certainly hated being denied the option when I was turned. But I can't see myself as a wife and mom. I don't want it. And if I don't want it now that it's a fucking miracle, I never will."

"Woman, your timing sucks," Sheena said. "Couldn't you have thought of all that before becoming human again? But then you'd have missed out on that threesome, so…"

So the subject was changed to something marginally less uncomfortable, as questions and comments were thrown my way. I answered a few, dodged many others, and soon I was half-drunk and giggling and thanking the powers that be for having girlfriends.

Me and the vampettes, *girlfriends.* Sheena, who handed us all to Willoughby, my best friend. Things changed from one day to the next. Hell, within a week, I'd gone from sleeping with both the men I loved, to talking to neither of them. I'd gone from vampire to human. Maybe I'd been too hasty to leave Alex. I might change my mind.

No. Breaking up with Alex was a good choice, and I shouldn't let insecurities change my mind. Even now, I missed talking to Constantine—in my dreams, in my head, and in reality.

Going to work did me good. It took my mind off things. Sally had to fly me in to Cecilia's photo shoot at the butt crack of dawn, because Sheena wouldn't hear of waking up that early. Cecilia was a darling. She was cooperative and took direction like a pro.

"Thank you so much." She wrapped me in a tight hug when the headshots were done.

Her hair was still long, but Sheena's stylist had given it volume, and it flowed and swung with grace every time she bounced on the balls of her feet. Which was a lot.

As she tucked it behind her ear, I saw a faint bruise on the side of her neck.

She saw me looking and covered it with her hand. "My boyfriend got a little overzealous. I tried to cover it with makeup, but…" She grimaced.

We could edit it out if it showed on her pictures, but I advised her to avoid this much passion in the future.

Trent called for her to change into a bikini for her body shots, and I spent the better part of the next two hours telling myself I looked great for my age.

I arranged for Trent to send the photos to Sheena, hugged Cecilia goodbye, and Sally and I took a cab to the agency. It was too late in the morning for us to fly. Sheena drove in, and Carrie brought my car. She and Sheena picked it up together with my stuff.

Alex was home when they showed up, and he was surprised not to see me. He asked them to tell me to call if I needed anything. It was nice of him. Alex was always nice, and I was a bitch for stealing the last few months from him.

No.

We'd been in the relationship together, both made mistakes, and now we went on our separate ways. Like mature adults.

God. I hated these mood swings.

The vampettes stayed with Sheena and me throughout another short workday, and then joined us for lunch and shoe shopping. It felt very *Sex and the City*, but in L.A. and with several of the ladies preferring a high-hemoglobin lunch. I loved my time with them and their efforts to keep me from thinking too hard about my life.

Work picked up from Wednesday on, with more appointments to juggle and companies to contact for Sheena. I got the hang of the computerized system, but Carrie dropped by once a day anyway. As did Sally. Liza had a catwalk in New York, so we didn't see much of her.

I stayed at Sheena's a few nights, enjoying the camaraderie and coddling of the other women, but being around them twenty-four-seven made me crave some space.

Finding an apartment on South Park was shockingly easy when I said the words *money is not an issue*, and the realtor Sheena hired for me had me moved into my own place before the end of the week.

By the way, I loved not having a budget, but I was also aware of the unfairness—the council had unlimited funds, but new vamps got a tiny nest egg. I should talk to Constantine about that.

Or not.

Alex and I exchanged a few texts. He was tired but good. He hadn't been sleeping well. We missed each other, but I said this was for the best, and he agreed. He reminded me I should get my final license plates, and I said I was on it. He said *good*. He insisted I should have the new stuff we bought for his place. Instead, I convinced him to buy off my share, and I spent the weekend shopping for my new sixth-floor apartment.

I had two large bedrooms, a kitchen, and a living room to furnish and decorate. And I had a *nook*—a bay window with a bench seat in my living room. I smothered it in pillows and lined the walls on either side with black-and-white photos of places I wanted to visit. I knew better than to think real plants would survive in my care, so I went with fake ones instead—all the beauty and none of the fuss. I wasn't up for a deeper commitment.

By Sunday evening, I was mostly unpacked and settled in, but fully exhausted and happy. Truly happy, in my open spaces and surrounded by bright colors.

I opened the last suitcase Sheena got from Alex's. Towels and sheets. No hurry to put those away; I'd bought new ones. I stuffed the suitcase in the back of my closet, to be dealt with another day.

I should have the girls over for drinks, to thank them properly for all their help, but not tonight. Tonight I'd enjoy my peace and quiet.

I poured myself a glass of white wine, put on some music, and picked up a book. An actual book. Romance, if you wanna know. The ceiling fan kept the room cool, but I opened the window and looked down at the lit street. I thought I saw movement to my right, and I swiveled my head, but there was nothing there.

If I'd never been a vampire, I'd say I imagined it, but my racing pulse hinted otherwise. I leaned out further, before I remembered I was no longer gravity resistant and would make a decent splatter if I lost my balance. I jumped back inside and closed the window, to be safe. If there was a vampire nearby, it'd be one of the vampettes, checking in on me. I should probably invite her in, but as I said—peace and quiet time.

* * * *

I started my week being all responsible and going by the auto dealership for my final license plates and the transfer of ownership. I think the salesman flirted with me, but I was in a hurry to get to work and really not interested.

Talent, old and new, paraded by the agency on a daily basis. My job was to log everything in, keep notes, and track their schedules. I also took it upon myself to take the arrogant, entitled ones down a peg or two. Most of them weren't a horror to work with, but Cecilia was the only one to bring us cookies—organic, low carb, and gluten free—and stole a couple minutes to ask about my day. No surprise that she was my favorite.

She visited a lot this week, to arrange for seminars, talk schedules with Sheena, or talk with her about a meeting, and she was always bright eyed and bushy tailed.

Which was why we were all worried to see her sad and exhausted when she came in on Thursday.

"You okay, hon?" Once Sheena decided you were one of hers, she was protective of you for life.

"Yeah. Sure." Cecilia sounded distracted.

"Is something wrong? You can tell us," I said.

Cecilia rubbed her eyes. "Had a long night. Nothing to worry about."

Sheena tapped her phone repeatedly. "You went out? I didn't have anything on your schedule for last night."

"No, no. I was home. Just stayed up late." She avoided our gazes.

My phone chimed with a text from Sally, who was across the room. I glanced at her, a *what the fuck?* in my gaze. When I read the text, I understood.

Should I mojo her for answers?

I shook my head. It was one thing to thrall our way into an early appointment, and another to use vampire powers to extract answers from someone against their will, on what was obviously a personal matter.

Cecilia looked no better the next day, and I happened to notice another bruise on the other side of her neck.

Okay, so I looked for it, but the point is that it was there, and I was no longer sure it was a hickey. I shared my finding with Sheena and Carrie, who was our designated undead babysitter du jour.

"So she's into kink." Sheena shrugged. "It's always the quiet, vanilla-looking ones."

But that's not where my mind went. "I don't think that's it. I mean, think about it. She's tired, moody—"

"She could be on her period," Carrie said.

"And the bruises? Nah uh. I think she has a vampire problem." Bet I impressed them with my mad deductive skills.

Sheena grabbed her tote and motioned for Carrie and me to get out so she could lock. "Because of two hickeys? You should be a mystery writer."

Carrie snorted. "Anything to take her away from the agency, huh?"

Sheena glared and took off down the stairs. Carrie hovered next to her, and I chased after them. "What was that about?"

"Nothing," Sheena said over her shoulder.

If I heard that again, I'd flip out. "Say *nothing* one more time, and I'm throttling you."

She kept going, while I hobbled on my heels three or four steps behind. "You can't say this is your dream job," she said.

"No, but—"

"I mean, you keep rolling your eyes at people."

"So do you," I said with more force than I meant to.

"I'm the *boss*, and you roll your eyes at me too, which is fine at home, but not at work."

I made it down to the ground floor with no shortness of breath and no ache in my knees. *Go me.* "You're right," I said. *Not* panting.

"And you're snappy. Bordering on rude, more often than not," Carrie supplied with a grin.

"Okay, okay. I get it. I'll be better next week."

Sheena rolled her eyes. See? "You won't be here next week. Surgery, remember?"

Right. I'd go up a cup size or two. Though I wasn't going with the double-Ds that would benefit my old career.

"I won't need the whole week; Sally said she'd help me recuperate."

Carrie scrunched her nose. "I'm not sure that'll be good. Implants are foreign objects. Vampire blood may make your body reject them."

Why didn't I think of that? "So I'll be out of commission for a few days."

Carrie cupped her breasts. "More like a few weeks, unless things changed since I got these babies."

I didn't know those were fake. "Weeks?" I caught myself stealing glances at her cleavage and raised my gaze to her face. "I don't want to be down for weeks. And if Sally doesn't heal the incision points, there'll be scarring."

"Then don't get the boob job," Sheena said.

Fuck. "I'll think about it. This being-human thing is losing its glamour day by day, though."

We stopped at the crossing, and I noticed a car at the street light. What looked like a very upset Cecilia was in the passenger seat, shaking her head and moving her hands animatedly. I couldn't make out the driver. "Hey, is that Cecilia?" I pointed at the car.

"Might be. She lives nearby." Carrie turned to look, but the light changed, and the car sped off.

"I think we should check in on her tonight," I said, breast augmentation taking a back seat in my thoughts. "Whatever is bugging her may be paranormal."

"Or she's having a difficult week with her boyfriend," Sheena said, leading the way toward the parking garage.

"And I guess by *we should check in on her*, you mean me?" Carrie harrumphed. She took out her phone and searched for something I couldn't see.

"I'll tell the girls you'll be late," Sheena said.

"Got Cecilia's address. I'll walk there. It's too early for me to fly after them." Carrie turned to me. "If it's nothing, you owe me big time."

"Totally." But I was thinking about my upcoming procedure again. Should I go through with it? Larger breast had been a dream of mine since I was out of puberty with my current set. Trying to make it in the adult-movie industry was a good excuse to bite the bullet and buy myself a pair, but my life had changed since. I had changed. And with how my back complained if I stood for too long, I doubted it'd thank me for the extra weight.

Or I was a wimp and didn't care for the painful recovery. Younger me was braver, stupider, or had a greater tolerance for pain.

I could live with that. And without implants.

Damn. Was this what maturity felt like?

Should I also try accountability on for size?

"Hold on, Carrie. I'll come with," I said.

Chapter Twenty

Cecilia didn't have a vampire problem. She had an asshole-boyfriend problem.

Carrie rounded the building and flew to the first floor windows, where she thralled a tenant to buzz me in. I waited for her, and we went up floor by floor, looking for Cecilia's apartment. Full disclosure—without Sheena around, I used the lift.

We heard yelling coming from a fourth-floor apartment, and I recognized Cecilia's voice. I was about to point out the door to Carrie, when she started banging on it. Made sense she'd hear Cecilia before I could. She was a vampire.

A guy yelled, "Go away," from the other side of the door.

Carrie mouthed *human*. When I whispered, "You sure?" she nodded and pointed to her ear and then the left side of her chest. She'd heard his heart.

I was searching for something to say that would convince him to let us in, when Carrie kicked in the door.

A shirtless human man in his early twenties was flung backward, yelling, "What the fuck?"

I followed Carrie in the apartment and saw Cecilia cowering at the corner of the living room. There was blood at the corner of her lip.

"You hit her." I wished I could rip him limb from limb.

"I'm going to kill you, bitches. You can't break into my—"

He didn't get to finish his sentence, because Carrie had him by the throat. She raised her arm, and his feet stopped touching the ground.

I rushed to Cecilia, and she averted her face.

"We're here to help," I said. "Has he hurt you anywhere else?"

She shook her head. "Not today. But you have to go. He has a gun."

I looked at the man, who kicked and thrashed. "Don't worry about him," I told Cecilia.

"Bitch. Let me down. What the fuck are you?" he yelled.

Carrie shook him and looked at me. "I need a catchy phrase, for when assholes ask that. How about, *your worst nightmare?*"

"Eh. Maybe, *someone who'll kick your ass*?" I asked.

Carrie grimaced. "I don't hate it, but… Oh, I know. We're the monsters under the bed."

This cracked me up, and I felt horrible, because Cecilia was trembling next to me. I gathered her in my arms and whispered, "I swear to God you'll never have to worry about him again. Believe me." I wished I had my vampire mojo and could thrall away her fear.

The man kept cursing and threatening us. He kicked Carrie in the face, and I winced. Now he was done for.

Carrie wiped her mouth with the back of her free hand. "You like hitting girls, huh? Helps you feel like a man? Does it make up for your tiny dick?"

He was weirdly quiet. I looked at his face, which was turning blue. She was crushing his windpipe and hadn't popped a fang. I was proud.

"Please," he squeaked and raked his fingers at her hand around his neck. "Please."

She punched him in the balls, and while he was crying with pain, lowered him so she could look him in the eye. "The moment I let you go, you're going to pack your stuff, take your car, and move to a different state. You will never contact Cecilia again. And every time you *think* of hurting another woman, you'll hurt yourself instead."

He nodded. He was cupping his balls but his face was slack, his gaze locked on hers.

"Go. Before I change my mind and end you right now." She dropped him, and he punched himself in the nose. Horrified shock etched on his features, he hobbled to the other room. When he reappeared, he was carrying a tattered suitcase. He didn't glance our way.

Carrie waited until he was out the door for good, and then she approached Cecilia and me slowly, like she didn't want to scare the cowering girl more. "Do I need to heal her?" she asked me.

I saw no wounds, and Cecilia's lip was no longer bleeding, but there could be internal damage. "Honey, are you sure he didn't hit you anywhere else?"

"No. Just a slap. I fell on the couch, and he pushed up my skirt, and then you knocked." She spoke dispassionately, like she was talking about someone else.

I remembered the feeling. "Cecilia, if you want, Carrie can make you forget all that happened," I said. "You can forget he ever existed."

Cecilia pressed the heels of her palms against her eyes. "I wish I could."

"You can." Carrie knelt in front of her.

When Cecilia lowered her hands, she no longer looked afraid, but determined. "I should remember. I should know there is such ugliness out there. And you... I don't know what you are, but thank you. You saved me today. And you saved the next girl too." She took Carrie's hand and squeezed. "Thank you."

Carrie grinned. "My pleasure. Totally. Just... if possible—"

"I'm not telling anyone," Cecilia said. "What would I say? That you're Superwoman?"

I offered to take Cecilia in for the night, but she said even with a busted door she felt safe at home now. Carrie made a call—she said it was to Sheena, but I had my doubts—and promised someone would be over to fix that door in an hour.

By the time I was tucked under my Egyptian cotton sheets in my heavenly double bed, in my super-amazing apartment, I knew what I wanted to do with my life.

I bet Sheena would be relieved when I told her.

I was too antsy to stay in bed after sunup. I got up and Googled what it took to become a licensed private investigator in California. Hmmm… lots of qualifications I didn't have. I knew who could help me acquire documentation, though. I waited until I wasn't risking Sheena's wrath, and made a breakfast run to the nearest bakery.

I called Sheena as I was pulling onto her street. "Hey. Can I come over? I'll bring coffee and pastries."

"Sure." She sounded groggy. "What time is it?"

I ignored her question. "I'll be at the door in five."

Sally got the door, and she and Sheena seemed not to mind the early visit. Carrie was asleep, and Liza was busy. Outside. On a Saturday morning. I suspected none of the girls had much of a life outside Sheena and the agency, and that was another reason they were always around. I wondered what Liza might be doing. Maybe she was visiting Constantine? Now that no women lived with him, she could make a move more easily.

Sheena bit into a Nutella-filled croissant and moaned. "After a week of healthy crap, this and a cup of java are a godsend."

"You're welcome," I said.

She arched a perfectly shaped eyebrow. "So you got your ass out of bed at this ungodly hour to bring us breakfast?"

I sipped my coffee and tried to look innocent. "Carrie told you about last night?"

"She did. Good catch. She said the guy was dangerous."

No mention of having Cecilia's door replaced. So Carrie hadn't called her. My PI-brain was on already. *Yes.*

"I think maybe this is something worth pursuing," I said.

Sally was playing with her phone. "Dangerous guys?" she asked without looking up from her screen.

"That too. Sheena, I'm sorry, but I have to quit. I'll still buy half of the agency, if you—"

"Praise the Lord." She laughed. "I adore you, you're my best friend, and I loved spending time with you, but you're a horrible assistant. Carrie had to go over all your entries remotely and fix your mistakes every night."

"She did? Why didn't you tell me?" I was too relieved, to sound indignant.

"You had enough on your plate. But what will you do for work? Or will you become a socialite instead?"

I closed my eyes, composed myself, and then opened them again and smiled. "I want to be a private investigator."

Sheena choked on her coffee and spat her mouthful back into her cup. "You wanna be what?"

"I wanna take weird cases that other PIs wouldn't touch with a ten-foot pole. I know the paranormal exists, so I'll have more options. And I'll need your realtor friend again. I wanna start looking for a place first thing Monday morning."

For the first time, Sally looked away from her phone. "Don't you have an appointment with Dr. K. Monday?"

"About that…" I chewed on my lower lip. "Not doing it."

"No lipo and no boobs?" Sally sounded shocked.

"No. I'll join a gym. Maybe."

"But you broke up with Alex *because* you wanted to have work done?"

"I broke up with him because I wanted the option. I wanted to be able to do anything I want."

She'd lost interest. She was typing things on her phone again.

"Thing is I need six thousand hours of paid investigative work the past three years, and I don't have them," I said.

"We can thrall someone for you," was her distracted reply. "Sorry, I need to put this post on my blog, and then I'll help you."

I gawked. "You have a blog?"

"Lifestyle," Sheena said. "She's promoting the agency through it."

"There. Done." Sally put the phone aside and smiled at me. "Who do we go see?"

"Alex or Constantine." I scrunched my nose. "I stupidly didn't get Ruby's number when she was here, and my mom has no way of contacting her, because Ruby doesn't want to leave a trail. But she's the only hacker I know."

"Tell me exactly what you need, and I'll get Constantine to ask her," Sally said.

And with that out of the way, I was out of excuses not to tell my parents of my current situation.

No, that didn't come out right.

It wasn't that I didn't want them to know I was human; I was afraid I wouldn't share their excitement at my news, when all I had to show was two lost lovers and a job that didn't fulfill me. Now I knew what I wanted to do with my life, it was easier to sound upbeat.

I still didn't do it face to face, though. After all, I was busy. There were classes to take and licenses to apply for and spaces to rent—and I wasn't sure I could look them in the eye when they asked how I was turned back.

I called that afternoon, and Mom answered. We exchanged the usual pleasantries, said we missed each other and I should visit soon, and then she asked, "How is Constantine?"

Umm…

Mom's radar was always on point. "Cherry, hon, is everything okay?"

I loved that she called me that. "Everything is fine. Mostly. Mom, I'm human again."

"Oh my God. *That's amazing.*" She yelled, "*Greg, she's human again,*" then in a quieter voice said, "How? And are you… Is everything as it was? Organically? Hell, I mean, there are no lingering issues from being undead?" She barely caught her breath between questions.

I smiled, though she couldn't see me. "Everything seems to be in working order."

"But how did it—?"

"Constantine found a ritual." No more details.

She laughed. "That man is our official benefactor—turning Ruby so she wouldn't die, helping you out with that man, and now turning you back and letting you stay with him…"

"I moved out. He won't talk to me, Mom. He said he doesn't want to watch me grow old and die. And Alex and I… We said we'd try to work things out, but we weren't compatible." I felt like crying. Apologizing for not wanting to give her grandkids. But this wasn't about her or anyone other than me. "He sees a big family in his future, and I don't."

The pause that followed raised my hackles, but when she spoke again, she didn't try to change my mind. "So where are you staying now? Do you want to come home?"

Her words warmed me up inside. "I'm renting an amazing apartment. You and Dad should come over. You can stay the weekend." I told her all about my color scheme and my view and my new career.

"Please be careful," she said. "There are all sorts of dangers out there."

It hadn't occurred to me that when I was a vampire they at least didn't need to worry when I went out alone at night. "I'll be careful. I promise."

We said our goodbyes, and I was about to end the call, when she asked, "Are you happy, baby?"

I gave it some thought. I was lonely, but I wasn't settling, and I was pursuing something I liked. "Most of the time."

Chapter Twenty-one

The vampires in my life came through for me again, and by Tuesday I had more than enough registered hours of investigative work.

Carrie accompanied me to get fingerprinted, sit for an exam, and submit my application packet. She used her gaze enough to make sure I wouldn't have to wait more than a week for my license, but she wouldn't help me get a firearms permit without completing the training course for real.

It took a month and a little help from my friends, but I had my office set up on the first floor of my building. It had a leather couch in the waiting room, and a huge mahogany desk with a winged desk chair in my inner sanctum. And a full bar, because PIs always served their clients alcohol in old movies.

The girls had insisted I needed a door like the ones in those movies, with a glass upper part and my name printed on it. I told them to go ahead and order one.

I saw the result at the unveiling ceremony, also known as *the first day we drank at my office*.

It read:

CHERRY STEM
Paranormal Private Investigator

The *Paranormal* part lead to a yelling match, with me saying nobody would take me seriously, and Sally insisting L.A. was all about the paranormal these days.

If it didn't get us clients, she said, she'd pay to have it taken out of the sign. And to print me new cards. Because I apparently had ten thousand of them as *Cherry Stem – PPI*.

Notice the *us* before? *If it didn't get* us *clients?*

I didn't give the word much thought at the time, but when I stumbled down the stairs the next morning, Sally stood outside my office door, dressed in all black and wearing sensible shoes, which up to that moment I doubted she owned.

And she had a tall latte in each hand.

She grinned and held out one of them. "Ready for our first day, boss?"

Come again?

I raised both hands, to show her I has holding a coffee mug and a set of keys and couldn't accept her offering. "*Our* first day?" I asked as I unlocked the door and walked in.

"Yup. I'm going to help you with this thing."

Saying I didn't need help would be lying, and I didn't want to hurt her feelings, but I wanted this to be my thing. Though it wasn't a horrible idea to have a vampire tagging along when I needed things done. "I didn't realize you wanted to be an investigator too," I said.

"Eh, modeling is cool, but it's not a long-term career. People will notice my appearance doesn't change. And I love to blog, but there's only so much experience I can gather by hanging with Sheena and the girls all the time. You, on the other hand, seem to know where to find trouble. You keep things interesting. And I'm sup—I like hanging out with you. So am I hired? You'll only have to cover meals and expenses." She waggled her eyebrows, and I wished for a scarf to cover my neck. Did she want to feed from me?

"Define *meals*," I said.

"Pizza? Chinese? Anything I feel like for lunch, whether we're at the office or working a case." Human food doesn't sustain vampires, but it tastes great, and for someone who'd been counting calories most of her life that was an amazing perk to going undead.

"You've got yourself a deal," I said.

"*Awesome.*" She wrapped her arms around me in an awkward hug, as she balanced the coffees. "I'm going to need a desk and a chair. And supplies. Do I use a company credit card, or—"

"*Sally.*" I glared.

"Never mind. I'll spend wisely, and you can pay me back when I return." Her glee was near-palpable, as she all but flew out the door, taking both coffees with her.

I should make her switch to decaf.

* * * *

"Any calls?" I cradled the received between my shoulder and ear and clicked on a pair of boots. They were stylish but seemed sturdy. Added to my shopping bag.

"Nothing since you last checked." Sally's reply carried down the line and from the other side of the door separating my office from the waiting area. "Wanna get something to eat?"

"No. I want a client." This was our daily routine for a fortnight now. We'd wait at our desks, play online games or shop, have lunch, wait longer, then go home.

I was bored.

I wanted to work.

To do *something*.

"Should we be like ambulance chasers?" Sally asked.

"Go to situations where people are guaranteed to have spouses cheat on them or business partners steal from them?" I infused my question with a healthy dosage of sarcasm.

"I was thinking more like go to haunted houses or look into unsolved mysteries." She tossed my sarcasm back to me.

I'd spent time with Sally when we both lived with Constantine, but not one on one. The more I got to know her now, the more I realized the airhead spiel was just that. An act.

Still… "We're not ghost busters. We're private investigators."

"*Paranormal* ones." She hung up, and moments later let herself into my office. "We need to play up the paranormal angle. People here love it. They believe in mediums and fortune tellers, and we're the real deal, Cherry."

I'd never seen a ghost, and as a human, odds were I never would. "*You're* the real deal; I'm in the know."

"More than anyone else has going for them. Let's get ourselves out there. I should write about this place on my blog. Get word out."

We already had that conversation and agreed it was better that her followers not know where she worked. Besides, investigative work had nothing to do with outfit-of-the-day posts.

"You don't need to worry about promo; I'm in charge of the administrative stuff," I said. Because I had to do something. This was supposed to be my newly found calling, but she had more ideas than I did.

"Well, administrate. Or let me? I'm so freaking good at PR, you can't even imagine. I'll have clients swarming in. Honest." Sally perched her cute butt on my shiny new desk. "Let me put an ad in the paper? It'll be awesome, you'll see."

"Okay, but I'm still the brains of the operation. You're the brawn."

"She said okay," Sally yelled.

Carrie showed up behind her.

I smiled, confused. "Hey. I didn't know you were co—"

"Told ya," Carrie said to Sally. She tossed a folded newspaper on my desk. "The ad ran today. Now we sit back and wait."

We.

"Did I hire you too?" I flipped through the paper, and sure enough, there was a half-page ad with my name in block capitals.

Beneath it, read:

Is a ghost haunting your house?
Do you suspect your boyfriend is a vampire?
Could your neighbor be a pet-eating shifter?
Whatever your supernatural problem, we'll kick its butt back to the hell that spawned it.

A nervous giggle bubbled up my chest and spilled from my lips. "Who thought of this?"

"I did." Sally arched an eyebrow. "And it's on my blog and Instagram too."

I tried to stop laughing, but I couldn't. Until I remembered the vampire council, and the laugh got lodged in my throat. "We need to take it down now. It has to disappear. If the council catches wind of this…"

"Oh, I'm sure Constantine will take care of it." Sally waved off my concern.

"But you don't know it. You haven't cleared it with him." Panic sent bile churning up my throat. "The council will have us all killed if they decide this might expose us. Expose you, I mean."

Carrie planted her hands on her hips. "Don't be a drama queen. It's no worse than any vampire movie. Those who already believe in us will see it as confirmation we exist. The rest will see it as a gimmick to bring in the gullible. And we don't say *we're* vampires. We say we know how to deal with them."

I forced my thoughts away from the gruesome scenarios running in my head. "Okay. We don't take it down. But you don't run it again either. Whatever happens happens."

"But Cherry—" Sally was probably about to protest my decision, but we'd never know, because the unimaginable happened.

My desk phone rang.

I looked from her to the phone and back again. If she was here, she wasn't calling me. Was it a potential client?

"Hel—Cherry Stem, Private Investigator." I didn't trust myself to say the *paranormal* part without laughing.

"I heard you take on cases others have no interest in." The male voice on the other end of the line was deep and smooth and reminded me of dark chocolate. And of Constantine. I hadn't thought of him much while I kept myself busy preparing my business, but his memory never stopped calling to an ache deep inside.

"What is this about?" I asked with as much authority as I could muster.

"It's a sensitive matter. I'd rather discuss it in person."

I wanted to tell him to please drop by *now now now*, and save us from the boredom of the past way-too-many days, but I pulled the threads of my professionalism together. "I'll connect you to my assistant, and you can arrange an appointment." I waved frantically at Sally, who flew to her desk, and then I realized I didn't know how to forward the call.

Carrie shook her head, her expression a mixture of exasperation and amusement. She came closer, grabbed the receiver, and said, "This is Ms. Stem's assistant. How may I help you?"

I listened to her tell the man we were very busy this morning but had an opening in the afternoon.

"Ms. Stem will see you at nine, Mr...." Pause. "Mr. Hunt. Thank you. Have a nice day."

"Nine in the evening?" I asked when she hung up.

She shrugged. "He said he has to work late but needs to see you today."

Chapter Twenty-two

Sally was gone when Mr. Hunt showed up, so I answered the door, and *damn*, he looked as delicious as he sounded. He was tall—though not as tall as Alex and Constantine—with dark skin and eyes a brown so light, they looked almost amber. His wide shoulders, narrow waist, and long legs were well defined by a designer suit, and I could see my reflection on his patent shoes as I introduced myself and invited him in.

The man was poise personified, with his elegant moves and perfect manners, but there was a sense of repressed energy coming from him. Like he hid a volcano beneath the sleek exterior. It made me think of Constantine again, and not because I missed him. Mr. Hunt hummed with power that didn't come with his lawyer career.

He followed me to my office and took a seat across the desk from me. I offered him a drink from my well-stocked bar, but he turned it down. His lips curved at the corners in a permanent hint of a smile, even while he described how his house was broken into and a precious stone stolen from him.

"Can you describe the gem?" I asked. "Any specific characteristics?"

He let out a chuckle that belonged in the Top Ten list of Sexiest Sounds Ever. "You'll know it when you see it. It's a sapphire, cornflower blue and two inches in diameter."

An alarm went off in my head. I doubted there were several stones that fit the bill, and last I'd seen one of them was in a dream, a couple months ago—a vivid, lifelike dream that almost cost me my unlife. And the queen bitch wore it around her neck.

If he was talking about that sapphire, odds were he either knew vampires were real or he was a jewelry thief. Either way, he wasn't *just* the big-shot lawyer he presented himself as. "Mr. Hunt—"

"It's just *Hunt*."

His last-name-for-first-name thing added to my suspicions. "Hunt, then. When you called, you asked if we take cases others turn down. It seems to me like the police would be able to help you with this. It's a straightforward burglary, and I'm sure your insurance will cover the gem."

"I didn't report the incident to the police."

"And why is that, if you're the legal owner?"

"Because there is no record of purchase for this sapphire, and whoever stole it wasn't interested in its monetary value, or they would have also taken the diamond bracelet that was stored in the same safe." He sounded calm and very much in control, despite basically saying he'd stolen the thing first.

"Do you have any idea who would steal it?"

"I suspect my wife's family. The stone belonged to her, and after Katje was gone"—his tone wavered for the first time—"they demanded I return it to them."

I wanted to comfort him, but the power he emanated filled the room, suffocating me. Was he a vampire? Was he thralling me right now? "I'm sorry for your loss," I managed.

He shook his head. "It was a very long time ago. But I need your help. You have to find the sapphire as soon as possible."

"I'll do my best. Can you tell me your wife's full name and any next of kin that live in the wider Los Angeles area?"

"Her name was Catharina Kappel. Her brother Filippus lives in L.A." He gave me the name and address, and I jotted it down, though the first place I meant to look at was Ádísa's old place. By vampire law, it had passed to her oldest childe, Constantine, and if I played my cards right, I might get to see him again.

"I'm prepared to pay anything to get the stone back," Hunt stood and produced a plump envelope from his jacket's inner pocket. "I trust this will cover the retainer and expenses for a few days."

He left the envelope on my desk, and I itched to tear it open and count the cash, to see how much this case meant to him. Instead I stood too. "Thank you, Mr. Hunt. I'll be in touch."

As I walked him to the waiting area, he said, "Would you have dinner with me this Friday?"

The cogs in my brain halted. If he was a vampire, he was dangerous. For all I knew, he was another of Ádísa's childer, out for blood. But then why wasn't he pouncing? He had to realize I was human now. He'd hear my heartbeat. His invitation had to be a trap, but if I turned him down, it might take forever to find out what he was up to.

Sally chose the worst day to leave early, damn it.

An idea slapped me full force, and I beamed a smile at him. "I'm busy Friday evening, but how about lunch, Saturday?"

As far as I knew, only Ruby's nearest and dearest vamps could move around during the day. If Hunt accepted the invitation and showed up, he wasn't one of the evil undead.

"I'm afraid I'll be out of town this weekend."

Of course. "Another time, then."

As I closed the door behind him, it occurred to me we never shook hands.

It was late, but I wasn't sleepy. Instead of going home, I locked up and went to my desk. I should call Constantine and ask for access to Ádísa's manor, but I needed to steel myself first for his negative reaction to hearing my voice. Maybe tomorrow… First, I was curious about the history of the gem. More so about how Catharina Kappel died.

An extensive search in public records came up with no results on her life or death. I tried *Catharina Hunt* too, and again got zilch, but if Hunt was a vampire, his wife might have been one too. Or she was never in the States, and he moved here after she passed. I looked for *Hunt* in California and decided not to bother wading through the pages of results. It'd help if I had a second name for him.

I could lift his fingerprints off the envelope and have someone run them through the system. Where *someone* equaled *Alex*. No. Bad idea.

Next time I saw Hunt, I'd shake his hand. See if he was warmer than room temperature. If he wasn't, I'd ask Constantine or Ruby to check the U.S. vampire census for me.

My eyes felt gritty. I rubbed them with the heels of my hands and checked my phone for the time. After three, and I had to be in at eight. The five floors to my bedroom seemed impossibly far. I made myself comfortable on the sofa in the waiting room and was out like a light before I thought to set an alarm clock.

I was startled awake by knocking. "Did you forget your keys?" I yelled, thinking it was Sally.

"I'm pretty sure you didn't give me any." That voice didn't belong to Sally or any other woman I knew.

"Hunt?" I glanced at the window and the sun sneaking in through the shutters. Daytime. Not a vampire.

I ran my fingers through my hair—never a good idea when your hair isn't straight, which I kept forgetting mine no longer was—and let him in.

He was dressed in tight jeans and a black T-shirt that defined every single muscle on his torso. He held up a carton with two coffee cups, and a paper bag from a bagel place I knew and loved. "Since you can't do dinner and I can't do lunch, I thought we'd settle for breakfast," he said.

I opened my mouth to respond but didn't know whether to thank him or say I was busy. I stepped back and waved for him to come in.

"Sorry, sorry. I have a good reason for being late. Honest." Sally squeezed in between us, rummaging through her bag. "I swear I tossed the keys in here this morn—" She froze, flared her nostrils, and turned to face Hunt.

"It's okay," I said. "Hunt, this is Sally. She's my receptionist-slash-assistant."

I expected him to offer his hand, but instead he returned Sally's expression, tilting his head to the side. The power I felt from him yesterday surged all around me, and I took a step back. Sally gave a light shake of her head and relaxed her shoulders. "Good to meet you, Mr. Hunt. I assume you're our new client."

I was glad she didn't say *first* client.

"Nice to meet you too." He gave a small bow. "I've only brought two coffees, but you can have mine, and there are enough bagels for all of us."

I thought of offering to go make a coffee at my place, but I didn't want him to know where I lived. I wasn't sure I appreciated his gesture. It was undeniably a little creepy.

Sally turned down his coffee, but she was more than happy to partake of the bagels, and was soon moaning over a corn-beef-and-mustard one with extra onion, while texting.

Hunt handed me my coffee, and I touched his fingers on purpose. He felt feverish. I withdrew more quickly than I meant to, and he smiled. "Everything okay?"

"Yeah. Let's eat here, and then I have a few more questions for you." I felt bolder with Sally around. My phone chimed. A text from Sally. This time I knew better than to look at her. I made sure Hunt couldn't see the screen, and I read her message. *He doesn't smell human. He has a heartbeat, but his scent is all wrong. Nothing I've smelled before.*

He definitely wasn't a ghost. A shifter? I thought they were near-extinct. I swiped back a quick, *Stick around.* I planned on getting to the bottom of this, and I needed some muscle, in case Hunt wasn't as friendly as he acted. My coffee was sweet and strong. "This is perfect," I told Hunt, as I stuffed half a bagel with cream cheese, lox, and capers in my mouth. "I forgot to eat last night."

He chuckled. "I like a woman with a healthy appetite." He was flirting with me, but I didn't feel any erotic interest from him. It was like he was going through the motions. Or he pretended to be attracted to me, to keep an eye on me, *because he wasn't human.*

We devoured breakfast, and then retreated to my office, where my desk acted as a buffer and a barrier between us.

I pulled in front of me the printouts of gems that matched his description, and flicked through them, to gain time as I gathered my thoughts. "*Ow.*" Paper cuts freakin' hurt. I brought my index finger to my mouth and licked the cut. Though my sense of taste had returned, blood tasted wrong. I splayed my hand and looked at the tiny beads forming a red line across the pad of my finger.

Hunt frowned, and I watched him watch my blood pool along the cut. "How much of a *paranormal* investigator are you?" he asked.

I frowned and licked my finger again. There wasn't enough blood to get Sally running in here, but better safe than sorry. "Not sure I know what you mean."

He stood and closed the door, and I opened my first drawer, ready to go for my gun. He rounded the desk, and I tensed, though his posture wasn't threatening. He leaned so close I could feel his breath, and whispered, "Do you know your receptionist is a vampire?"

My first reaction was to laugh, but I schooled my face into an impassive mask. "I know. I don't know what you are."

He sat down again, no longer bothering to keep his voice low. "She'll probably tell you, but I'm a shifter. Panther."

Of course. I should have known by the sleek muscles and feline grace. "I've never met a shifter before. Should I be afraid?"

"Not of me. Others may take offense in the company you keep."

"Others? I thought you were all… gone."

He gave me a half-nod, half-shake of the head that meant nothing.

When I was with the VSS, Constantine told me shifters and vampire were non-mixy, but since there were a handful of shifters left in the world, I didn't expect it to be an issue. "And what do you want from me? For real, this time."

He sat back and crossed his arms. "I really want you to find that stone for me."

"What about the rest of your story? Did you even have a wife? I found no record of her in the States."

Sadness darkened his eyes. "She existed. Part of her still does, which is why I need the sapphire. Katje and I met at a different time, when magic… Never mind. Vampires and shifters were enemies, and though I had no ties to sever, her maker and his other childer opposed our mating. For centuries"—so shifters were immortal too?—"we ran and hid from them, as well as from bigots who hated our other differences, but fifty years ago her maker found us. He trapped the part of her soul that loved me, along with all her memories of me, in one of four soul sapphires."

Four. And one of them had been around Ádísa's neck in Alex's dream.

"Am I boring you?" Hunt asked with the same smile that wouldn't leave his lips yesterday.

"I'm sorry. It's a lot to absorb."

"And there is more. Last year, I tracked down her brother in L.A. and stole the stone, but I couldn't use it until I found where they kept Katje. I stuck around, in case he had her with him, but I've never seen her enter or exit his house. A few days ago, someone started following me. I don't see them, but every now and then I feel a presence nearby. Then, day before yesterday, the sapphire disappeared. I need to find it and find my mate. I need to make her whole again." His voice broke.

"I'll help you," I said. "We'll find them both." Someone around here deserved a happily-ever-after, damn it.

Chapter Twenty-three

Sally came in without knocking. "I couldn't help but overhear..."

I arched an eyebrow.

"Okay, so I listened in. I want to help, and I'm sure the girls will be on board. They need the distraction. Constantine too. The more the merrier, right?"

"You're a vampire," Hunt said. "Why help?"

Sally batted her eyelashes. "I'm a sucker for a good love story. Do we know how many vampires will be at the brother's house?"

Hope softened the hard angles of his face. "Two that live with him. A couple others that come and go." He frowned. "I just realized you're out in the daylight."

She opened her mouth to answer, but I cut in. "You have your secrets, we have ours."

Shit. I shouldn't have said *we*. I felt his scrutiny like a physical weight. To divert him, I asked, "Why were you flirting with me, if you're so set on finding your wife? Why the dinner invitation and the breakfast?"

"I had to know whether you were a hack or the real thing, so I meant to stay close."

As I imagined.

Sally asked Liza and Carrie over. While we waited for them, I left her and Hunt talking about the layout of Filippus Kappel's estate and went to her desk, to call Constantine. Sally could have done it, but I wanted to hear his voice. I missed him, okay?

"Cherry." His greeting lacked emotion.

"Hi." Now I had him on the line, I didn't know what to say.

"Is this an emergency?"

"It may be council business."

"I'm listening."

"I have a were-panther in my office." Which might make more sense if Constantine knew what I did with my life. "I'm a private investigat—"

"I know. But a were-panther? I was led to believe—"

"Yeah, me too." If he could interrupt, so would I. "I didn't ask him to shift or anything, but he says that's what he is, and I believe him. The thing is he's mated to a vampire, and her… *kiss* I think it's called? Anyway, they locked away the part of her that loves him in a sapphire like the one Ádísa had in Alex's dreams. A soul sapphire?"

Constantine cursed, and hearing him lose his cool was soothing. The cold version of him broke my heart.

Like I broke his.

"You've heard of soul sapphires?" I asked.

"I have, and I feel like an imbecile for not recognizing it when I saw it. I believed she haunted Alex's dreams because of who she was before she became a vampire. I didn't think…"

"This isn't about her. She's gone, and we need to help Hunt and Katja."

"Your new shifter friend and his mate? What can the council do for them? Are they registered in the U.S.? We have no authority over European vampires."

"I don't know. Can't you check the census? Please?" After Ádísa and Johnny-boy's deaths in our hands, the council decreed a census, to record all vampires in the United States. Even if the Kappels weren't registered as natives, we might find useful information about them. Like whether Catharina was in the country.

He let out a tortured sigh. "You realize you're still a council member. You could do the research yourself."

"I'm trying to stay under the radar. If one of the others decides to drop by and ask why I'm looking into things, they'll know I'm human."

"I hate when you're right, but I'll look into it. Have your Mr. Hunt call me tonight. If the council can't help him, I will."

"What about me?"

"You will not get involved." His tone brooked no argument. "I will not have you risk your precious humanity." He spat out the last word like it had a foul taste.

"This is my case. You can't tell me what to do."

"I know. But if you want my help, we do it my way." He hung up, and I felt empty.

Hearing his voice for a couple minutes wasn't enough. I needed to see him—touch him. I couldn't. I went to the small WC and splashed water on my face, then studied my reflection. I'd changed my hair back to red this month. It felt more *me*. There were black circles under my eyes, but I looked good. Self-assured. Like I knew what I was doing.

Ha.

I went back to my office and found Sally and Hunt laughing.

"Your assistant-slash-receptionist is a delight," Hunt said. "She has given me hope I can be with my Katja once again."

I told him about my call to Constantine.

"Another vampire willing to assist?" Hunt's expression was a mix of incredulity and suspicion.

"If the Kappels aren't registered with the vampire council, this is vampire business," I said.

"Is Katje in danger, if she's found in the country unregistered?" he asked.

I hoped not. "Constantine will be in charge of the case, and he'll make sure she's safe. I trust him with my life."

"Plus he's a big softy deep down," Sally said. If Constantine ever heard that, there might be an evisceration in her near future.

Hunt stood and all but crushed me in a giant hug. "I will owe you forever," he said.

I wouldn't be around that long.

Carrie and Liza joined us, and I stayed and tossed ideas for a Plan B with them. If the council couldn't intervene, they'd have to storm Kappel's place. Deep down, I hoped Constantine would drop by and help with the planning. He didn't.

By 1 p.m. my lids were drooping and my temples throbbed with the beginnings of a headache. Another thing to add to the *con* list for being human.

"I need a shower, a nap, and some downtime. Call me if you need me, otherwise forward calls to my cell and lock when you're done," I told Sally.

"Sure thing, boss." She didn't glance my way, too engrossed in her discussion with Hunt and the girls. She was so excited, I smiled despite myself.

I had my usual fight with the water temperature, but managed a semi-decent shower and was under the covers in no time. My new sheets were crisp and cool and inviting, but sleep wouldn't come until I took some ibuprofen for the pain.

Even then, Hunt's story, my relationship with Alex, and my brief talk with Constantine rattled in my head. Hunt and Katje made it work despite ignorant racists and lethal supernaturals, and I couldn't commit to a wonderful man who wanted a future with me. I was honest when I told Alex

I didn't want the same things out of life that he did, but I finally admitted to myself he was right too. It was also about Constantine.

I was supposed to get over him, but I thought of him whenever I had a moment to myself. Like now, when I should be sleeping.

I squeezed my eyes shut and willed away the thoughts. It must have worked, because the next thing I knew was an incoming text waking me up.

Unsurprisingly, it was from Sally.

Forwarded incoming calls to my cell, so you'd rest. Hunt called. He dropped his wallet at the office. He can be there in an hour, and I'm busy. Will you get it for him?

I looked at the time. 8:15. I'd slept the afternoon away. I couldn't bother typing, so I pressed *Call*, but she declined my call and sent, *Can't talk. Hunt will fill you in.*

I got dressed and went downstairs to wait for him and see if I could find anything online about soul sapphires.

Hunt was on time, and I let him in and handed him his wallet. "Sally said you'd fill me in," I said. "Do you have a plan?"

He nodded. "I spoke with Constantine. He didn't find Katje's family in your council's records, but his search unfortunately raised a red flag. Enforcers went to Filippus' estate at sundown. He has forty-eight hours to leave the States peacefully. They found two more vampires with him, but no sign of Katje. Constantine and Liza will break into his place tomorrow during the day, to look for the stone. Carrie and Sally will help me lure whoever's shadowing me, and use them to get to Katje. I'm not losing her again."

His determination again brought to mind Constantine—not that he was ever far from my thoughts these days. "How did you make it work for centuries?" I asked.

He smiled. "We built a relationship that suited us both, and we never let external factors get between us. If we needed space or a diversion, we took it, but we talked about everything. And had regular, passionate intimate moments."

I only half-smiled, because my next question weighed on my chest. "After all these years, are you sure she's alive?"

"We're mated, Cherry. When she dies, so do I."

I was trying to wrap my mind around the love and certainty it took to tie your lifespan to someone else's, when I heard glass breaking in the inner room. I rushed to see what happened, but the moment I opened the door to my private office, someone rushed me.

My attacker was too fast for me to see a face, but it was a woman, judging by the shrieking and the breasts pressing against mine, as she body-slammed me to the floor. She yanked my hair aside painfully, baring my neck.

I looked up in horror, as fangs descended toward me. In that moment, I forgot my training. I forgot how to move. I forgot how to speak. I lay there and waited for the furious blonde to rip into my throat.

As if the night wasn't surreal enough, a low growl came from my left. The vampire on top of me froze, and I followed her gaze to a huge beast prowling toward us. It was a panther, almost twice my length and black as midnight, its coat sleek and its yellow eyes shining under the overhead light. The clothes Hunt wore were strewn in tatters behind him.

I hated being the only human in the room. Also, could shifters tell friend from foe when in animal form?

The vampire, who I strongly suspected was Katje, narrowed her eyes at Hunt and hissed. She sat back, and as the panther leapt for her, I kicked her off and rolled on my stomach, to crawl away as fast as my trembling limbs allowed.

"Get off me, mutt," Katje screeched. Hunt had her cornered, and she flailed and scratched him. Why didn't she toss him across the room? Huge or not, he couldn't weigh more than a car, and vamps can lift cars.

I found my phone, miraculously unscathed despite my landing on my ass, and called Sally.

Can't talk, she texted again, after cancelling my call.

Vampire attack at the office, I wrote back. I should get out of there, but I watched in sick fascination as the animal lowered its jaws toward the woman he loved. I squeezed my eyes shut, not wanting to see him kill her, but when she shrieked again, it wasn't in horror but fury.

Hunt said, "You smell different."

I opened my eyes and saw him pressed against her in all his naked man-shaped glory. He sniffed her. "Look at me, Katje. Remember me. I'd never hurt you."

She screamed for him to leave her alone and raised welts on his back with her fingernails, but he wrapped his arms around her and held on.

"Don't touch me." Her screams had faded to pleading. "I don't want you near me. You mean nothing to me."

"Then why did you follow me here? Why attack this woman?"

"*I don't know.*" The yell broke into a sob. "I can't get you out of my mind since I saw you at my brother's house. You sneaked in and stole my sapphire, and I need it back."

"Were you the one following me?"

"I wanted to kill you"—she was crying in earnest now—"but I couldn't bring myself to pull the trigger. Why can't I kill you and get you out of my system?"

"Because you love me."

These crazy kids would have their happy ending after all, and I was intruding. I convinced my legs it was time to stand, and was reaching for the handle when I heard Sally say, "Wait. I have a key."

Constantine broke down the door. He rushed the huddled couple, and I yelled for him to wait, but Carrie and Sally managed to hold him back. He fought to get free, but Liza grabbed his face, and they span him to look at me.

"She's here. She's fine," Liza said.

Constantine had a wild look in his eyes, that tonight were the dark blue of stormy sea. Was all this pain and worry for me?

"Constantine…" I took a step toward him, and the vampettes let go, but he slid his impassive mask over his features.

"You're all right. Good," he said. "Now if you'll excuse me, I'll have to retrieve the sapphire tonight, if we're to save this woman's sanity. Liza, join me?"

I reached for his hand as he passed by me. I expected him to avoid my touch, but he gave my fingers a tiny squeeze before walking out the ruined door.

Katje was thrashing under Hunt, trying to throw him off, denying the truth of his words.

"Will she be safe if we get you both to your place?" Carrie asked Hunt.

"I have built a room that will detain her until she can be restored," he said.

"Good. Sally, help me?"

The two vampettes held Katje still until Hunt got on his feet. He was very naked, and his clothes were unwearable.

"I'll see if I have something you can wear," I said. Five minutes later I was back with a tracksuit that was too tight and short for him but wouldn't get him arrested for indecent exposure.

Katje oscillated between threats and pleas, but the three of them managed to get her outside.

"Do you want my car?" I asked.

"Better to fly them," Sally said. "Something tells me she'll be a horrible passenger."

"Call me when it's all over?" I kept away from the unstable vampire snapping her jaws at me.

"I will," Sally said.

"Let Sheena know where we are," Carrie told me. To Sally she said, "Ready?" and all four of them took off toward the night sky.

Chapter Twenty-four

I bypassed the mess that was my office and went straight home, to call Sheena. "Drinks while our vampires save the day?"

"Cherry. Hey. Everyone okay? Sally said you were attacked." She sounded like she was crying. Was she afraid something happened to me?

"We're all fine," I said.

"Good. I was worried." But she didn't sound relieved; she sounded like shit. "Did it have to do with your case?"

"Yeah. How much has Sally told you about it?"

"I know a gorgeous were-panther is looking for his bespelled vampire bride and a sapphire that holds her soul or something." Her tired voice belied her humorous words.

"Well, the vampire bride came after me, and the shifter grabbed her," I said. "The gang is going to get the jewel tonight, so you and I can have a slumber party while we wait for news."

"Nah. I'm tired, and you could use some rest."

I wouldn't take *no* for an answer. She needed the company, and so did I, if I were to stop thinking of how Constantine ran to my rescue and then took off instead of talking to me. Constantine never fled from anything. "If you don't come over, I'll come to you, and then you'll have four of us all up in your space tonight," I told Sheena. "Come *on*. We'll order in, and veg out in front of the TV. I'll even let you sleep in tomorrow."

"I don't know..."

"*Please?*"

"Okay. But no chic flicks."

I ordered a couple of huge, greasy, calorie- and fat-ridden hot dogs with bacon, mustard, and extra relish, and fries. Praise the Powers that Be for all the stair climbing, or I soon wouldn't fit in my jeans. I added a salad, to assuage the guilt. There was beer and white wine in the fridge, and I found *Fast & Furious 6* on Netflix.

Sheena looked exhausted when I let her in. Her eyes were bloodshot and sunken.

"What happened?" I asked as she threw her arms around me.

"Me? You were the one attacked."

"My door and window got the brunt of it." I studied her face. "What's the matter, hon?"

"Nothing. I'm tired. There's never any quiet around the house."

"Now tell me the truth."

"I am." She looked away.

"Are you sick? Is your wound acting up?"

She shook her head and met my gaze. "I'm fine. A friend passed away earlier today. I knew it was coming, but I miss him already."

My pulse thudded in my ears. Sheena didn't have many friends. "I'm sorry for your loss." I hugged her, and a niggling fear tied my stomach into a knot. "Was it someone I knew?"

"Have you talked to Constantine recently?" Why did she change the subject?

"I saw him today. He broke down my door, saw I was okay, and left. Didn't even look at me. But he knew I'm a PI, when I called to ask about this case. Guess the girls told him."

"Guess so. Did he seem well?"

She was leading to something my brain refused to puzzle out. "Yeah, except for the wanting-nothing-to-do-with-me part." My heart was racing, but she'd tell me if there was something wrong with him.

Sheena rolled her eyes. "He loves you. You chose not to be with him; he gets to choose not to be your friend."

The intercom buzzed, and I jumped before I remembered the hot dogs.

I got the door and returned with an armful of drool-worthy artery cloggers. We got some food into our systems, and then drowned our sorrows while watching sexy people wreak havoc.

Sheena yawned, and I paused the film to go make the guest bed for her. The king-size sheets I bought when I moved in were too big for the queen bed in the spare room. I was resigned to tucking in a lot of fabric, when I remembered I had the right size covers in the suitcase stashed in my bedroom closet. As I tried to pull out a set without laying the suitcase flat and opening it all the way, a folded piece of paper slipped out and floated to the hardwood floor. *Alex* was scribbled on it, in Constantine's handwriting.

It was Constantine's note to Alex, and Alex wanted me to have it.

It took me three tries to pick it up; my hands shook.

"Need any help?" called Sheena from the living room.

"I'm good," I called back and opened the note.

Alex,

I never expected to consider you a friend, but I do, so I mean it when I wish you and Cherry a long, happy life together.

This woman is my world, however, and should you ever hurt her, I will become your worst nightmare. Letting go of her is only possible because I know she'll be happy with you. If she's not, let her free. Cherry isn't meant to fit in the norms you were brought up to embrace. If she chooses to do so, make it worth her while.

Be good, my friend. Be healthy. Be happy.

Sincerely,
Constantine

Tears fell from my eyes and soaked the paper in my hands. I felt lightheaded and sat on the bed, rereading the note.

"Is this from him?" Sheena asked from the doorway. "Did he tell you about Wesley?"

I snapped my gaze to her. "Wesley?"

"Shit. Constantine made me promise not to tell you."

"What happened?" That came out shrill.

"The last of Wesley's great grandkids passed months ago, and Wesley decided he didn't want to live any longer. He passed away tonight."

"Oh God. Poor Wesley." The tears came harder.

"He asked us not to cry for him." But tears beaded her eyelids. She blinked them back. "He had a full life, and it was his choice. He stopped taking Constantine's blood about when you came back from your parents."

I wiped my face. "Constantine's blood?"

"That's what kept Wesley going. How else do you think he got to live almost a hundred and eighty years, and still be spry?"

I sniffled. "I didn't know. I thought he was old, not *old* old." Because I never cared to ask. Because I was too absorbed with my drama to get to know the gentle old man who took care of everyone. "I didn't even know that was possible." *Someone* could have told me when I was a vampire dating a human.

I'd miss Wesley. He was ancient—literally, apparently—but I never thought of him dying. He was a constant in my life and in Constantine's. "Constantine…"

"It destroyed him. Between losing you and waiting for his closest friend to pass, he became a hermit. When we went to visit Wesley, Constantine made himself scarce. This case is the first the girls saw him in weeks."

"Why didn't any of you tell me? I wanted to say *goodbye*."

"Wesley said you did, and Constantine didn't want you to return to him out of pity. He wanted your new life to be filled with happiness."

I remembered Sally telling me I should go to him. That we were both alone. "Doesn't he know Alex and I broke up?"

"Carrie called him when we found out—sorry, but we're his friends too—and when she mentioned you, he stopped her and said he only wants to know if you're in trouble or need help."

Stupid, stubborn man. "But he knew I was a PI."

"Which none of us told him."

I shook my head. "I'm sorry. A good man is dead, and I'm making it all about my nonexistent love life."

"Wesley would be happy if you and Constantine made things work," she said with a sad smile.

"Too bad that's not gonna happen, huh?"

She came to sit next to me. "Hon, you know your situation isn't irreversible, yes?"

"He said he doesn't want to—"

"No, woman. I mean you don't have to stay human if you don't want to."

Be a vampire again? Did I want to? Would Constantine turn me if I asked?

But did I want to?

"Do you love him?" Sheena asked.

"Yes, but I loved Alex too, and—"

She didn't let me finish. "Do you love being human?"

"I don't hate it. It's cool, I guess, now I can tell flavors apart."

She gave me a light smack upside the head. "Focus. Do you love being a human?"

I thought about it. Being human was about growing, experiencing all stages of life, and not outliving everyone you forged a connection to. With the exception of Sheena and my parents, my nearest and dearest were all undead. Humans could walk in the sun, but with Ruby's brew, so could vampires, and they didn't get period pains or migraines or hunger pangs.

"What if one day I decide I want children?" I asked.

"You adopt. Or you take the girls in. Or get a dog."

I thought of the night I shared with Alex and Constantine. The choice I made that night wasn't between the two of them; it was about the life I craved. I loved Alex—I really did—but I didn't choose *him*. He was the added bonus.

Would I do it all again? Yes, because I needed to see what I'd missed out on.

Would I make the same choice today?

I planted a kiss on Sheena's cheek. "Thank you."

"I won't wait up," she said, kicking her shoes and making herself comfortable on my bed.

Chapter Twenty-five

The Uber dropped me off at the mansion's gate.

I considered pressing the intercom button, but my inebriated brain insisted it was better to climb the wrought iron fence.

Using the gate for support and the strength-boost alcohol afforded me, I lifted my weight up the end post. My jeans didn't offer enough friction, and my hands hurt. It took several tries, and I berated me my stupidity the whole time it took to reach the top. My relief when I swung my right leg over the top rail was squelched when one of my belt loops got snagged on the spike behind me and I couldn't move either way.

Screw it. I'd call Constantine, and if he left me hanging—literally—I'd threaten to call 911.

I pulled out my phone, but my fingers were clumsy and sweaty with the effort it took to get up here. The phone slipped through them. I watched horrified as it landed on a rock and the back jumped off, spilling out the battery and sim card.

Awesome.

"*Constantine*," I yelled. "Hey! Help me down. Your stupid fence has taken me hostage." He was a vampire. He should be able to hear me.

Sometime later, I realized he couldn't. As far as I knew, he was still out, looking for the soul sapphire. Fuck.

I don't know how I managed to fall asleep in the most uncomfortable position imaginable, or how the jeans held my weight and saved me from plummeting to the ground when I half-slid off the iron rail I straddled, but Constantine's face was inches from mine when he said, "What the fuck are you doing, Cherry?" His expression wavered between amused and angry. And maybe concerned?

"Waiting for you?" My eyes burned again. I was supposed to throw myself in his arms and profess my love. Instead, I was dangling upside down like meat at the butcher's, and I couldn't figure out where to start. I looked around. I was on the inner side of the fence. I'd count that as a win.

He helped me down and handed me the remains of my phone. "What do you want?" he asked, holding the gate open for me to exit.

I leaned my weight against it, but his grip kept it from closing. "I need to talk to you," I said.

"Is it another case? The girls can help you. My part in this one is done. Kappel's place was empty when we went in for the sapphire. Since he didn't follow protocol, he's a fugitive in the U.S., so I expect he left the country. Hunt will apply for Katje to stay legally. He'll call you."

"Thank you, but that's not why I came."

"Why *did* you? I've repeatedly asked you to keep your distance." He glowered, violet and grey swirling in his eyes and confusing me.

"I'm sorry. About Wesley, not for being here. Sheena saw me crying, and she thought I knew. He was a good, decent man, and I'm so sorry he's gone." I cupped Constantine's face, but he shied away from my touch.

"I'm tired, Cherry," he croaked. "Tonight I lost the best friend I've had in centuries, and I ran to do your bidding before his body was cold."

"I didn't know—"

"I'm tired of hurting." He trapped me between his body and the gate. "I'm tired of missing you and being lonely, and I'm tired of you not getting that seeing you and not having you is torture."

"But—"

"I don't want to hear how you miss me too and want us to be friends. I don't want to be your friend. I want you to leave me alone."

"Constantine, I love you."

He huffed. "But not enough. Why do you torment me? Are you enjo—"

"Oh, will you shut the fuck up?" That shocked him into silence long enough for me to add, "I'm not here to torture you. I love you enough. I want to be with you."

He widened his eyes and took a step back. "Best case scenario, I can delay your aging, but I can't watch you wither away like Wesley. I won't do that."

Was he always this dense?

"No, you insufferable man. I want to be a vampire again, and I want you to be my maker."

He leaned in close, and I closed my eyes, thinking he'd kiss me. Instead, I heard him sniff. "You've been drinking," he said. "You don't know what you're saying."

I glared. My thoughts had never been clearer. "I'm not drunk. I want this as much as you do. Unless you're not that into me when I'm actually available."

"And what does Alex think about this?" Constantine asked, his voice dripping honey all of a sudden.

"Alex and I are done."

"That's why you came back. We're interchangeable for you. It didn't work out with one, so you'll scurry to the other. I told you before—I won't be the consolation prize."

How could he love me and be such an ass about it? I poked him in the chest hard enough to hurt my finger, though it had no effect on him. "I broke up with Alex weeks ago, because I don't want a family. I tried to be human, but I didn't like it. I tried to live without you, but you're the only thing on my fucking mind. Now, will you get over yourself and kiss me already?"

I didn't expect it to work without further groveling, but he snatched my finger and pulled me into him. An electric current ran through me when our lips met. How did I ever survive without him?

He deepened the kiss, and I felt lightheaded. My feet no longer touched the ground. Constantine flew us across his gardens, kicked down his own front door, and took me to his bed.

He wasn't gentle with my clothes, ripping my jeans in two and tearing my T-shirt off me. "Forgive me, but I've waited too long. Too long."

"Don't worry. I have other clothes," I said, fighting to pull his shirt over his head.

He snapped the elastic in my thong and pulled down his jeans without unbuttoning them. "Foreplay next time. You have my word." He pulled me to the edge of the mattress by the ankles, lifted my legs in the air, and slid inside me in one long thrust.

This. This was what I needed. Not a hard cock, but the connection with Constantine. Feeling him inside me. Spreading me. He draped his body over mine, folding me in half. My legs dangled over his arms as rammed into me time and again.

I arched up to find his lips and breathed into his mouth. I didn't know if my human body could withstand the way he contorted me, but I didn't care.

He folded one of my legs around his hips and splayed his hand over my chest. "Are you sure you no longer want this?"

It took a second to realize he meant my heartbeat. "I'm sure." I bucked against him, urging him deeper. Faster. I wanted him to take me to my limit. To throw me over the edge. To end me and breathe new life into me.

His skin was cold against mine, but he scorched me when he palmed my breasts and squeezed, using them to drive his thrusts. He hurt me in the most delicious ways, and I couldn't wait till I was a vampire and could take more of it. More of him.

"It doesn't have to be now." He punctuated each word with a thrust. "We can have a romantic evening. Candlelight. Strawberries. Chocolate. I want to make it special for you this time."

"You're all I need," I whispered. "Don't ever stop fucking me."

"Not planning on it anytime soon." He kissed me again, plunging his tongue into my mouth as he pumped his cock inside me, hard and demanding.

I bit his lip with enough force to draw blood. It drove him wild. His rhythm became punishing, and I thought I'd faint with pleasure.

My body tightened around him, and I felt the ball of fire in my belly prepare to erupt. I tossed my hair to the side and swept my hair out of the way. "Now. Please."

Constantine kissed along my jaw line and down my neck, while he inched his hand toward my cunt. He pierced the flesh with his fangs at the same time he pressed his thumb on my clit and twisted.

I came apart. My legs thrashed of their own accord, as my heart pounded in my chest. I dug my nails in his shoulders, and felt the skin give way, but I didn't care. I latched on to him and rode out my orgasm, as I felt my life's blood fill his mouth and trickle to pool on the sheets under my head.

Constantine wedged an arm under my shoulders to hold me close. He kept fucking me and drinking me down, prolonging my release while he drove me to yet another death.

I slid into darkness like more than once before, but this time I didn't panic. I was where I belonged.

"I love you."

Epilogue

I open my eyes, and smile when I see Constantine's beautiful face. He's lying on his side next to me, one leg between mine. The darkness does nothing to hide him from me, but brings out his beauty in stark relief. I take in his sparkling eyes. His generous lips. His perfect teeth. The angle of his prominent cheekbones. With his halo of golden hair, he could be a wicked angel.

"Good morning," he says. His eyes are their normal light blue and no longer look haunted.

"Mmm…" I stretch and bring my fingers to my neck, where he bit me—was it this morning? "What day is it?"

"You were only out a few hours." He runs his fingers through my hair. "I love this color on you, but you were just as fetching when you went blonde. I was being a jerk when I said otherwise."

"Thanks." If I were human, I'd blush. I'm not, so I blow him a kiss. How did I ever stay away?

"You came back to me." For an older-than-dirt vampire, he has the boyish grin down pat.

"And you were a bastard about it." I tease the light sprinkling of hair below his navel, and his cock bumps against my hip.

"I didn't expect you to change your mind, especially after you got your own place and made the effort to register as an investigator."

I sit up and look down at him. "Sheena said you wouldn't let anyone talk about me. How did you know?"

He squeezes his eyes shut. "I may have checked in on you once or twice."

That's rich. "You *checked in* on me, when I wasn't allowed to call you? You're horrible." I bat his shoulder, but I'm grinning. If he hadn't insisted on keeping his distance, I might have settled for having him around, and we'd remain in limbo.

He clasps my hand and places it on his chest. "Maybe once a week, tops. I had to know you were okay."

"So you knew Alex and I broke up?" I ask.

He turns his gaze to my bare breasts. "I did. I didn't know why, though."

"And this morning you threw him into the conversation because…"

He rakes his fingers through his hair and sighs. "I had to know if you were choosing me, or if I was all you had left."

He knows me better than that. I should be upset, but it's comfy here, and I don't need to pee, and I can eat anything I feel like and never take the stairs anywhere again, and we're both naked, and I'm happy.

Truly very happy.

"Round two?" Constantine asks, as I say, "I'm keeping my apartment and my job."

"Sure," I reply, as he says, "Whatever makes you happy."

He makes me happy. And he makes me happier by kissing and licking his way down my body, teasing, pinching, and nibbling until I beg him to eat me out.

Which he does. With gusto. Then he bites my inner thigh and drinks from me again.

Later, I'll ride him to oblivion and feed from his neck while he whispers my name like a prayer.

At some point I need to get out of bed and check my phone. It rang a couple times during the day. Might be Hunt. Sheena knows I won't be back for a few days. She'll tell Sally, but I have to call Mom and Dad and update them on my situation.

I should talk with Constantine too. If this is going to work, we must do it right this time. I'm keeping my place, though I don't mind spending every night with him. And he can help me with my PI-ing. If we change our working hours and vet clients properly, we may even get council sanctioning.

At some point, I should tell Alex I'm a vampire again. We're not together, and I owe him no explanation, but I want him to know he did nothing wrong. I just wasn't cut out for mortality.

Constantine stirs beside me. The man is insatiable, and I match his appetite. I straddle him and rub my wet slit along his shaft.

Without opening his eyes, he says, "You'll be the end of me."

No, wait. He didn't move his lips.

Euphoria spills through my veins, making my nerve endings tingle, and he's not even touching me. *"Can you hear me?"* I ask in my head.

He looks at me, startled. "Shouldn't I?"

I send, *"I didn't speak."*

I feel my joy fill his chest. I feel my weight on top of him. I feel my slickness against him. He bucks his hips and enters me, and I'm both of us at once.

"I love you." The thought is in my head, but I don't know if it's mine or his.

I'm happy. I'm whole.

I'm home.

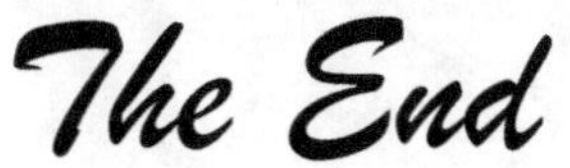

The End

(but you should keep reading)

Later the same night

"I knew you'd find your way back to him."

I snap my head toward the foot of the bed and see Wesley's simmering form smiling at us.

I squeal and pull the sheets over my naked body. Constantine jumps up and looks around in alarm, but his gaze glides over the specter now hovering next to me.

"He can't see me." A hint of sadness tinges Wesley's voice. "You've died more times. You're closer to us."

"To… ghosts?" I blink, and he turns brighter, making the rest of the room fade behind him.

"Cherry? Who are you talking to?" Constantine grabs my arm and shakes me. In my head, I hear, *"If someone's haunting your dreams—"*

"It's okay." I meet his gaze long enough for him to see I'm awake and aware of my surroundings. "It's Wesley."

Constantine starts to ask more, but I shush him and use our mental link to project to him what I saw.

"How are you here?" I ask Wesley.

"My unfinished business was to see Master Constantine happy. Now I can rest. Thank you. Take care of him for me." He cups my cheek, and I feel his touch, but when he tries to straighten the candle on the nightstand, his fingers pass through it.

"I will," I say. "Thank you for everything."

"Goodbye, my friend." Constantine sounds as choked up as I feel.

Wesley brightens into a ball of pure white light, and then dissolves into a million sparkles that disappear before they hit the floor.

"So now I see ghosts, apparently," I say.

Constantine sits back wide eyed and gathers me to him. "Apparently."

If only that were the last of the surprises coming our way.

We've got a whole week to ourselves, before Alex calls the mansion. It's not about me.

Constantine asked Ruby to look into soul sapphires, and she's enlisted Alex's help. Don't ask me why.

According to her, there aren't four soul gems, but ten, and they're not all sapphires. Their original name was *Petradia tis Anamonis*, which translates to *stones of waiting*, and they put things or people into stasis.

I think they're no more real than the Excalibur, but Constantine believes there's more to them. He's afraid Ádísa's essence is still trapped in one of them, and we're not done with her yet.

We'll go check her place tomorrow, and then look into Willoughby's last known residence, but I don't expect to find something.

Upside to this phone call was that Alex seems fine with me and Constantine being together. We said we'll all have drinks when he comes home.

Here we go again, with the freaky civility.

I should write a book about these guys.

Keep reading for the first chapter of
Cherry Stem and the Pissed-off Ghost

In the past, I let my undead status hold me back, but not anymore. After all, a vampire is perfectly placed to run a paranormal detective agency. Right?

The problem is my latest client is dead. And pissed off. And with a severe case of memory loss.

Constantine and Alex—the immortal love of my unlife and my human friend with benefits—want to help, but I'm the only one who can see the dearly departed, and that puts me in the eye of the storm.

Also, did you know there's another plane of existence out there? Well there is, and it's missing a couple lethal shifters.

Just when I thought I was done with drama...

Chapter One

There are days when I crave coffee more than I crave blood. This was one of them.

I took a sip of my cappuccino and sighed. Perfect—both the cappuccino and the quiet.

Well, the café wasn't technically quiet, it buzzed with people chatting, but nobody was talking *to me*. After a day of Sally at her most upbeat, this was bliss. I mean, there's no law against vampires having a sunny disposition, but the girl can be more excitable than a poodle.

Speaking of… A white furball ran up to me, rose to its hind legs, and started pawing my shin and yipping.

"Hey, you." I let it sniff my hand, and it wagged its tail and gave me doggie kisses, but started barking again when I tried to pet it.

"Mom, he's here." A little girl appeared behind the mini poodle. She stopped inches from my table. "He likes you," she said to me.

I *am* likeable.

"He's adorable." I gave the dog a gentle nudge, so he'd stop scratching at me, and returned to my coffee.

A woman about my age—which is now thirty and will stay that way for all eternity, *thank you very much*—knelt and picked up the dog. She held out her free hand, and the girl took it. "You should leave the lady alone," the woman said.

"Oh they're not bothering me." I gave her a genial smile.

Mistake.

The woman pulled out a chair. "I'm so happy to hear you say that. Can we sit with you?" She helped her daughter climb on the seat and planted the dog in the girl's lap.

I looked around. All other tables were taken. "Sure," I mumbled.

"You won't even know we're here. I'll grab a coffee and be right back. Mind keeping an eye on these two for a few?" For the second time, she didn't give me the chance to answer. She was off, and I was left with a grinning little girl.

I took out my phone and sent Alex, *Where are you? I'm being accosted by a kid and her dog.*

Be there in twenty, he sent back.

It was already eight thirty. He was supposed to be here now. *Hurry. I'm getting hungry*, I wrote.

My phone buzzed almost immediately. *Don't bite either of them.*

I was typing, *No promises*, when the girl said, "You're pretty."

Maybe I wouldn't bite her.

"Thank you. You're pretty too," I said. She was. She had her mom's dark eyes and olive skin, and long wavy hair pulled up in twin ponytails.

"I'm four, and I can count to ten-two."

What was I supposed to say to that? "Okay." I opened my phone's browser. I'd saved a few You'd-Never-Believe-This articles, and maybe the kid would leave me alone if I looked busy.

"I'm Michaela. This is Nibblet. He's a Maltese."

So that was a *no* on the leaving me alone.

I smiled.

"What's your name?" Michaela asked.

"Cherry."

"Like the fruit?"

No, like the porn star I wanted to become once upon a time, but it might not be legal to share that with a minor. "Exactly," I said.

Her mom returned with two cups. One smelled like coffee, and the divine scent of hot chocolate wafted to me from the other. If I extended my vampiric sense of smell, I could tell how much sugar was in each cup and whether the chocolate had whole or skimmed milk in it, but then all other scents in the establishment would assault me, and I wasn't in the mood for unwashed-armpit odor.

I nodded and returned to my screen. From the corner of my eye, I saw the woman pull out a magazine.

"My mom is Karla," Michaela said. "Mom, this is Cherry."

Karla and I exchanged awkward smiles. "Don't bother the nice lady," Karla said, without looking at her daughter.

"My mom is a lawyer," Michaela said. "What is your job?"

I obviously couldn't avoid her. I looked at my coffee. It was the perfect temperature. I could gulp it down and go wait for Alex outside.

The eagerness in the girl's eyes kept me in place. She wanted to talk, and her mom was too busy or too tired to indulge her.

"I'm a private investigator," I said. Which was true even if I had no clients.

Sally was optimistic and insisted work would pick up any day now. Her exuberance was what made me keep *Paranormal* in my job title long after the trial period she and I agreed on. It was also what got me up and to the office most mornings. Well, that and my determination to not be absorbed by my relationship this time around. I was my own woman and had my own interests. And one day maybe a job that was more than a hobby.

"Like a detective?" Michaela asked.

"Just like one." Only my target group was people with supernatural issues. And a couple of ghosts I'd helped tie up loose ends, though not by choice. It came with the territory of being the only one I knew who could see them.

Michaela clapped her hands. "Then you can help me find my teddy bear."

I could brush her off or explain that I didn't find misplaced teddy bears, or I could play along. I was in a charitable mood, because it was Friday and Alex was coming home with me.

"I can try." I fished a pen and my leather-bound pad out of my Balenciaga bag. The pad was a gift from

Constantine—flashy, cherry-red, with my name and *Paranormal Private Investigator* emblazoned in the spine in gold. I loved the thing; it was his way of saying he was proud of me for taking charge of my unlife. The pen was one of those dime-a-dozen ones because I never met a pen I didn't chew on. "Describe the bear to me."

Michaela climbed to her knees on the chair and leaned on the table, dropping Nibblet on the floor.

The dog yipped furiously, until Karla gathered him to her, not looking up from her magazine. Either the article was super interesting, or this was her first break in days.

"Mr. Boggles is a very special bear. He sings to me at night, and he watches over me. Daddy said so." Michaela's eyes were big as saucers, her face serious.

I thought Karla rolled her eyes, but it was hard to tell for sure. "Can you tell me how big he is? What color?"

"He's this big." The girl opened her arms wide. "And brown."

This was a lot to go on. Not.

I tapped my pen on my open palm, and then chewed on the cap, looking at my notes.

"Do you remember where you last saw him?" I asked.

"On the couch, next to me."

"And when was that?"

Karla mumbled something about Michaela leaving *the lady* in peace, as the kid counted fingers. "Seven days ago."

I narrowed my eyes. "You sure you didn't take him somewhere with you?"

Michaela shook her head. "Mr. Boggles never leaves the house. He's an indoors bear. That's why I'm so worried about him." Her chin wobbled.

Her mom had probably thrown out the toy. "Is there anything else you can remember?" I asked.

Michaela shook her head again.

"Did the bear have any characteristic marks?"

Another *no*.

Karla huffed. "One of its eyes is missing. Nibblet must have gotten to it, because it was a gaping hole when I found it. I sewed the edges together." She sipped on her coffee.

"So will you find him?" Michaela turned huge brown eyes on me.

I reached for her hand, and Nibblet growled at me. I ignored him. "I'll do you one better," I said. I held Michaela's gaze and deepened my voice, using my vampire mojo to influence her. "You will forget all about Mr. Boggles." I don't usually thrall people unless I'm threatened, physically or with exposure, but this was a tiny nudge that would save the girl some pain.

Her mom looked at me, startled, and I took the opportunity to thrall her too. "You will get her a new teddy. And make sure you spend actual quality time with her whenever you get the chance." Movement outside the window caught my eye, and I saw Alex's Chrysler pulling up. I stood and left a fifty on the table. "Actually, get her the bear from me." I was gonna have a *very* good afternoon and an even greater night or two. I was all for sharing the happiness.

I slipped into the passenger seat and laid a quick kiss on the corner of Alex's lips. "Hey, you."

"Hey." He tilted his head toward the coffee shop and the window table I'd just vacated. "Making friends?" His smile said he remembered I didn't do well with kids. I don't hate them, and I used to babysit for a friend at my old apartment building—until said friend was abducted and almost drained because of me—but I'm not a fan, as a rule.

"The coffee shop was crowded, and they had a cute dog," I said. "Long day at work?"

He stepped on the gas. "We had a Jane Doe in a dumpster. Not pretty. Gonna need full facial reconstruction."

I grimaced. Nothing like a messy murder to kill the mood, and I knew firsthand how horrible being disposed of in a dumpster was.

I still tried to salvage what I could. "Have you eaten?"

"A sandwich, a million years ago. Hope Blondiebear's latest little helper has made actual people-dinner."

I laughed. "I'll pay you to call Constantine that to his face."

Alex grinned. "I don't have a death wish. Seriously, though, tell me he found someone who can cook."

Since his friend and butler passed, four months ago, Constantine had been going through one maid service after another. Nobody could fill Wesley's shoes, after he'd been with Constantine for more than a hundred and fifty years. And yes, he was human. Regularly imbibing vampire blood can prolong human life.

Which was why Constantine and I sneaked some into Alex's meals whenever he joined us at the mansion. Don't judge. We care.

"We'll order in," I said.
Alex chuckled. He looked better than when we were a couple, and it wasn't the vampire blood. His smile reached his eyes these days, like when we first met. It was good to see.

Acknowledgments

Thank you, Allyson Lindt and Sofia Grey, for sticking with me throughout Cherry's journey, holding my hand, and helping me up when I stumbled. I couldn't have finished it without you. Thank you, Milana Jacks and Camilla, for loving Cherry and her boys and asking for more when I felt too overwhelmed to write. Thank you, Andrei, for reading it over and over when I was sure I'd messed up, and for all your solid advice. And for putting up with me when I'm on writing sprees. I love you.

Last but not least, a great big thank you to everyone who's followed this series to the end. I hope you give my other books a chance, and that when I'm ready to return to Cherry's world, you'll make the leap with me.

About the Author

Sotia loves romances with a twist and urban fantasy novels, always with vivid erotic elements. Her favorite characters to write are not conventional hero-material at first glance, and she enjoys making them fight for their happiness.

She shares her life and living quarters with her husband, their son, and two rescue dogs, one of which may be part-pony. Sappy movies make her bawl like a baby, and she wishes she could take in all the stray dogs in the world.

Also, she hates mornings!